How had Wyatt found her? And why?

"Autumn?" he said as he cocked his head. "Do you own the dog boarding and training business?"

She shot him a tense nod in answer to his question.

"Doc Earl mentioned you were looking for a part-time dog trainer." Though his spine was straight and shoulders at attention like they'd likely taught him at basic training, something about his posture was off, kind of defeated, which made her wonder what hardships he'd endured since they were together.

"Yes," she answered. "Why?" Baby raced back to her and leaned against her leg. The terrier whined, sensing her owner's agitated state. Autumn picked her up, this time clinging to her for emotional support.

"I'm a certified dog trainer." He slid off his Stetson and held it against his leg.

Uh-uh, she would not work with Wyatt.

Because having Wyatt here would be a daily reminder of the time in her life that she wanted to forget.

T0197899

Heidi Main writes sweet inspirational romance novels set in small towns. Though she lives in central North Carolina's suburbs, she dreams of acreage and horseback riding, which is why her novels include wide-open ranches and horses. Before starting her writing career, Heidi worked with computers and taught Jazzercise. A perfect Saturday is lounging on the deck with her husband and watching the many birds in their backyard. Learn more about her books at heidimain.com.

Books by Heidi Main

Love Inspired

A Nanny for the Rancher's Twins
A Family for the Orphans
Her Loyal Companion

Visit the Author Profile page at LoveInspired.com.

Her Loyal Companion

HEIDI MAIN

LOVE INSPIRED
INSPIRATIONAL ROMANCE

LOVE INSPIRED®
INSPIRATIONAL ROMANCE

Recycling programs for this product may not exist in your area.

ISBN-13: 978-1-335-93672-1

Her Loyal Companion

Love Inspired
22 Adelaide St. West, 41st Floor
Toronto, Ontario M5H 4E3, Canada
www.LoveInspired.com

Printed in Lithuania

MIX
Paper | Supporting responsible forestry
FSC® C021394

Come unto me, all ye that labour
and are heavy laden, and I will give you rest.
—*Matthew* 11:28

To God be the glory.

Rich, thank you for supporting my dreams in every way possible and being a constant encourager. I can't express how much that means to me. So a heartfelt thank you, sweetie.

Shado, again thank you! You are my go-to gal for farm and ranch information. Yay, we got a Jack Russell terrier as a main character!

Teresa Motley at Raintree Jacks, your dedication to rescuing Jack Russell terrier dogs inspires me and many others. The idea of rescuing instead of purchasing a puppy resonates with me. Your operation sparked the idea of having Autumn train rescue dogs instead of raising puppies to become service animals, so thank you for inspiring that unique twist for my story and for saving little white dogs.

Chapter One

Autumn McCaw drew in a comforting breath of hay and rough-and-tumble dogs, thrilled to finally be part of something she believed in. Tori and Zoe, her five-year-old twin nieces, chased each other around the haphazard hay bale maze she'd set up as a training test for Tallulah, the female Portuguese water dog she'd rescued a few months ago. The screams, shouts and quick movements were exactly what she wanted to test the dog on. Like Tallulah had been taught, she sat at attention, her eyes solely on Autumn and not the rambunctious girls. Success! She'd been training the medium-size black dog in basic obedience and social skills so she'd be ready to become the amazing diabetic service dog Autumn knew she could be.

Laney entered the little barn that Autumn rented from their neighbor, Henry Wright. "Girls, quiet down," her sister-in-law said as she cradled her hand around her seven-week-old baby boy positioned on her chest in a front carrier. The identical twins abandoned their running and screaming to hug their mother. Tallulah gave the newcomer a quick glance and then trained her eyes back on Autumn.

"Thanks for letting me borrow the girls. They were perfect," Autumn said. With a hand motion, she released the dog and walked her to the nearby outdoor pen where a couple of other pups frolicked.

"I'm glad they could help. They were up early enough this morning." Laney chuckled. "Tallulah seems to be doing great." Her eyes danced. Since she'd started her own business recently from the ground up, she knew how important this venture was to Autumn.

Baby, the Jack Russell terrier Autumn had adopted right before she'd returned from Dallas, jumped at her knees. She picked up the smooth-coated sweetheart and pressed her to her chest, always happy to have her loving dog close by.

"I'm thrilled with Tallulah's progress," Autumn said. "Now if only I could find a dog trainer so my eager clients can get their promised service dogs." She had assured Barbara that her son, Tanner, would have Tallulah by the time he went to summer camp in two and a half months. If she didn't find a trainer soon, she'd have to call Barbara and backtrack on that date and Tanner would be heartbroken. Autumn knew the basic obedience and social skills she had taught Tallulah wouldn't make a service dog, but she had to do something to move the dog's education forward while she waited for a trainer.

"We've been praying for God to provide just the right person to help you," Laney said. Then she gave Autumn a quick hug and corralled her girls to head home.

Would God bring that person? Or was Autumn's dream of connecting trained dogs with people in need not important enough for Him?

With her past, she wasn't sure.

Autumn heard the crunching sound of gravel grinding beneath tires and moved to the wide doorway to see who had driven into her parents' spacious parking area below.

Baby squirmed in her arms so she put her canine companion down.

The dog barked and raced down the hill toward a vehicle she didn't recognize. Thankfully, Henry's barn was on the edge of his property, overlooking the Triple C Ranch, so it was convenient for the McCaws to walk over anytime. And superconvenient for her because she had moved back in with her parents while she got this venture up and running. The big truck came to a stop, and she racked her brain for who it could be. She didn't have any appointments scheduled and her parents weren't home.

The newer-model four-door truck with an extended cab parked, then all the windows rolled down before the occupant emerged. The man fitted his Stetson on his head and walked toward her, glancing back at his vehicle every few steps. As he neared, she caught sight of his face and sucked in a breath at the familiar man striding toward her. Wyatt Nelson.

His well-worn work boots ate up the gravel drive between them, but what caught her attention was the dejected look on his sculpted face. As he neared, her stomach tightened at all the memories that flooded back.

They had had an unforgettable day together seven years ago, followed by a night that went further than either of them intended. But the ensuing six months, and the emotionally painful ending to her unexpected pregnancy, had changed the course of her life and left her reeling from shame and regret.

Wyatt's snub for not acknowledging her multiple voicemails and text messages had hurt and confused her. To make matters worse, the massive secret she'd been withholding from loved ones had created a chasm between her and her family that distressed Autumn.

She licked her dry lips. How had Wyatt found her? And why?

When his gaze landed on hers, he startled, as if he hadn't expected to see her. For a moment, his steps faltered, but he kept moving forward. He ran his hand over his barely there facial stubble, drawing her attention to his strong chin and chiseled cheekbones.

"Autumn?" he said as he cocked his head. "The vet clinic owner didn't tell me. I mean, do you own the dog boarding and training business?" He squinted up at the hand-painted business name above the entrance, then peered past her as though searching for the actual owner.

She stiffened. Why did he find it absurd for her to own a business? She shot him a tense nod in answer to his question.

"Wow, okay, so Doc Earl mentioned you were looking for a part-time dog trainer." Though Wyatt's spine was straight and shoulders at attention as they'd likely taught him at basic training, something about his posture was off. He looked kind of defeated, which made her wonder what hardships he'd endured since they were together.

"Yes," she answered—she was desperate for a dog trainer.

The last time she'd seen Wyatt, he'd been at a small island resort to attend his best friend's wedding and hadn't appeared to have a care in the world. At least, not until he'd received an emergency call that his grandmother was in the hospital. He'd taken the next flight out and she hadn't heard from him since. Which was fine, really it was. When they'd met, she'd just gotten out of a lousy relationship and wasn't looking for another one. So when she and Wyatt had immediately connected, she'd been concerned, but he'd assured her he had no intention of anything long-term either. Relieved, she had enjoyed their brief time together. But when he'd left the island, she had missed his companionship. Probably more than she should have.

He glanced back at his vehicle again. What concerned him about his truck, which was only about fifty yards from where they stood?

"What are you doing here?" Baby raced back to her and leaned against her leg. The terrier whined, sensing her owner's agitated state. Autumn picked her up, this time clinging to her for emotional support.

"I'm a certified dog trainer." He slid off his Stetson and held it against his leg.

Uh-uh, she would not work with Wyatt. That'd be uncomfortable. No, more like awkward, thorny, impossible.

She hoped the swarm of emotions warring inside her weren't readable on her face. She stuck her nose into Baby's fur and prayed for peace. Yes, she'd been looking for a certified dog trainer for months, to no avail. Everyone expected a salary and, with a brand-new business, she couldn't afford to pay anyone, especially since she'd had start-up costs. That's why she was offering the apartment above her parents' garage in exchange for the work.

"You're with the military, right?"

As he loomed over her at well over six feet, his ramrod straight shoulders seemed to straighten even more. "Mostly stationed in San Antonio. I was a K9 trainer almost the whole time I was in the Air Force. Trained dogs and handlers." He roughed a hand through his high and tight military hair. "I just separated from the Air Force after twelve years of service and moved to Serenity to be near family. I snagged a job as a vet technician for Doc Earl at Mighty Paws Vet Clinic."

Ugh, if he weren't Wyatt, he'd be perfect for the job. Baby laid her chin on Autumn's shoulder, reminding Autumn that her dog was here for her, which eased her anxiety a notch. The terrier had entered her life when she had needed emotional support to get through the day, and Baby had naturally filled that gap. Years later, Autumn had taken Baby to get her official emotional support dog certification. During those classes, this business idea had taken hold.

"I don't think working together is the best idea," she said.

He peered toward his truck and frowned but didn't disagree. Gratitude swooshed into her core. She was glad he understood.

Satisfied with whatever had him concerned in the parking area, he turned and shifted to see around her. "Your facilities look nice."

"I'm happy with what I've accomplished so far." She hugged Baby a little tighter, promising herself she would not show him around. In fact, she should kick him in the shin for ignoring her in her time of need. Instead, she chose not to make eye contact.

"Doc Earl said you just opened a couple of months ago. I see you have boarding clients already."

She tried not to take his comment to heart, but she was pretty pleased she'd gained a bit of traction so early on. These boarding clients would help fund getting trained dogs into the hands of people who needed them.

Probably sensing Autumn had relaxed a bit, Baby wiggled out of her desperate grasp and ran through the dog barn toward the outdoor pens.

"Nice crates," he said as his gaze swung to the barn and her kennel setup, but his demeanor said something else. Like he was judging her, maybe? No, she was just reading into things.

His gorgeous chocolate eyes remained focused on her facility, presumably taking in the symmetry of the shiny new enclosures, the smaller ones stacked on top of the bigger ones.

A fancy cage that looked like a piece of furniture specifically for the clients who wanted their beloved pet to have a larger, more homey space flanked the wall of crates on each side. Bales of hay sat against the other wall for seating. She had purchased these crates for a super low price, and the clients who had toured the space had commented about how new and clean everything looked. The four boarded dogs barked and pawed at their enclosure.

"Thank you, I love it." She answered his praise. "But I'm looking forward to getting the service dogs I've already promised trained." If only she hadn't bitten off more than she could chew by assuming she could mimic some online training videos. But shortly after she'd promised the dates, she had realized she'd need a certified trainer if she wanted to do the dogs justice.

She shook off her gloomy thoughts and took in the boarding facility she'd created from a dusty and unused barn. Since he was semi-retired, Henry no longer used this as a hay barn, so he was happy to let her use it. She had cleaned up the place, purchased dog kennels, built roomy outdoor play pens and started the boarding portion of her business.

Now she needed a trainer to start the exciting part. One who wasn't named Wyatt Nelson.

But she had no other prospects. Not a one.

In the warm spring breeze, she glanced at Wyatt, two years older than her twenty-eight, if she remembered correctly. Since the moment he had left the island, she had struggled to forget him. Was her struggle because of their immediate connection or the secret she'd tried to suppress for years?

"Why dogs?" he asked. "I thought you were in sales or something?"

Why hadn't he fessed up about not answering her calls and texts when he first arrived instead of creating this awkward situation between them?

"I've had lots of jobs." She shrugged away her years of testing out different occupations because when she adopted Baby and experienced how much the dog changed her life, Autumn's passion had surged. "When I learned the difference between emotional support animals and service dogs, I felt called to provide service dogs to people in need."

A quick flash of approval crossed over his face. Of course he agreed with her business plan, because training dogs was his life.

He dug the toe of his boot into the gravel. "I wish you'd reconsider, Autumn. My daughter and I won't be a problem, I promise."

She sucked in a breath at the news. "You have a daughter? How old is she?"

"Harper. She just turned four." With that pronouncement, the discouragement and strain on his tanned face morphed into fatherly pride, an expression she'd seen on her older brother's face repeatedly. A slow smile took over his features and his tense eyes warmed, reminding her of their captivating time at the resort. Once again, he peeked over his shoulder. What in the world was he looking for?

"And your wife?" She paused, waiting for the answer.

A shadow passed over his face before he aimed his attention at the ground. "She left us. It's why I had to leave the military and, um, move away. Long story." That dejected look claimed his features again. Her chest ached at the broken marriage and the little girl involved. "Listen, Autumn, working for free rent is perfect for my situation.

Doc Earl said it's a one-bedroom?" His masculine frame filled out the brand-new polo shirt with the vet clinic insignia on the right pocket.

"Yup. Right above my parents' garage." She pointed in the direction he had come. She'd been praying for a dog trainer, someone who'd work in exchange for rent, and here was Wyatt, desperate to do just that.

Triple C Ranch Dog Boarding and Training would never grow without the dog training element she planned to offer, and someday the rancher she leased the barn from might decide he wanted her to pay for this facility.

Yes, she and Wyatt had a history, and she really didn't want him around the Triple C, but maybe they could help each other.

The problem was, if she hired Wyatt, let him and his daughter live at the Triple C, she'd have to deal with her painful past.

Because having Wyatt here would be a daily reminder of the time in her life that she longed to forget.

Wyatt Nelson eyed the oversize garage, waiting for an invitation to view the apartment. But instead of being hospitable, Autumn gathered the terrier she'd snuggled with earlier in her arms and ignored him. He found that odd because seven years ago, he'd been drawn to her kindness. Her wide smile and gracious disposition were the reason he'd asked her out on a date. But today she wasn't being very kind to him.

As cows mooed, he breathed in the pleasurable aromas of dog and hay. It surprised him how comforting he found the town of Serenity, and what he'd seen of the Triple C Ranch felt like home. How could he get Autumn to consider him for the job?

On the island where they'd met, he and Autumn shared one memorable afternoon, followed by an equally memorable night. He had never forgotten her. But he hadn't been interested in a relationship because of the lies and deceit his father had served up to Wyatt's kind and trusting mother. Autumn had been the first woman to tempt him, and that had scared him.

"Daddy," Harper shouted.

He looked over his shoulder at his daughter shutting the dual-cab truck door and then waving at him. Relief swept over him that Harper hadn't become worried when she awoke in the truck alone. He'd made sure he was in her sight line the whole time he'd been talking with Autumn, but lately she'd been fragile.

He grinned and beckoned her to join him. She started racing up the hill, but stopped when she saw enticing dandelion puffs at her feet. She crouched, plucked a dandelion and then blew the white floaties into the air and beamed while they floated away.

"Is that your daughter?"

"Yes. Harper."

"You can leave your kid alone in a car?" Autumn tugged her dog closer. In response, the terrier laid her snout on her owner's shoulder.

"She was sleeping when I arrived. I lowered the windows and stayed in sight, so when she woke up she'd see me."

"Well, at least it's a cool day," she said, as though judging him for poor parenting skills.

"She's four, and perfectly capable of unbuckling from her booster seat and getting out of the truck by herself," he said, hating the defensive tone that crept into his voice.

Autumn's gaze bounced between him and his daughter like she was watching a tennis game. Her honey-blond hair hung in waves, highlighting her pretty face. A curious expression covered her features while the cute dog licked her cheek and then watched Autumn as if worried about her owner. Wyatt wondered if the terrier was an emotional support dog. If so, what had happened in Autumn's past to necessitate a support animal? He shook off the notion. Something about being a dog trainer always had him thinking too hard on dogs' actions.

After Harper finished climbing the hill, she moved to his side, pressing close. New places made her shy, but he hoped if he got this job and apartment, that she'd acclimate to the Triple C.

Autumn turned her attention to his daughter, then dropped to her knees. The observant dog stilled in her arms. "You must be Harper." His daughter smiled, not her usual response to strangers. "I'm Miss Autumn and this is Baby."

Harper fidgeted, but didn't step away.

"You can pet her. She loves children."

Harper put her hand out and the terrier licked it. His daughter giggled, an authentic giggle that melted Wyatt's insides and gave him hope that her mother's thoughtless actions had not permanently scarred her.

"Can I see our apartment now?" Harper whispered.

Surprise crossed Autumn's face. "Maybe later, okay?"

Harper nodded right when the dog jumped out of Autumn's arms to run across the grass. His daughter followed with glee, and just like that, her shyness evaporated.

He was relieved, because she rarely warmed up to people or places so quickly.

Autumn stood and gazed at Harper rolling on the grass. Or maybe she was concerned her support dog had left her. "I don't think we should work together—"

"Can I see the facilities—" They spoke at the same time.

She frowned, glanced at Harper, then shrugged. "I guess." As she moved into the barn, she seemed a little less anxious than when she'd first spotted him. She gestured at the wall of crates he'd seen earlier, explaining she'd adopted three dogs to turn into service dogs and had reserved the rest of the enclosures for potential boarders.

"For a barn, this space is spotless. I can see why your dog boarding venture took off so quickly."

Her cheeks pinked at the compliment. "It's helped a ton having Earl recommend me."

Her words about how they shouldn't work together were stuck in his head. Maybe she was right, because her cold shoulder made no sense. They'd parted on good terms, right?

Seven years ago, when his grandmother's health scare was over, he'd returned to San Antonio and his life. The phone he'd used at the resort had been a prepaid international phone, so he wouldn't be hit with fees. He'd almost given in and called her a couple of times so, to remove the temptation, he'd thrown away the disposable device. Part of him regretted not saving her contact information, the sane part knew if he had, they might have become an item and he hadn't been ready for that.

Autumn tucked a lock of hair behind her ear, a worried look covering her face. Had she tried to reach him and became frustrated when she realized she didn't have his Texas number? Nah, the way she'd been treating him spoke volumes. Clearly, she hadn't thought of him since they had parted ways.

They moved out the back entrance. She stopped and pointed at the barn. "Our neighbor, Henry Wright, owns this structure and has been kind enough to let me use it at no charge."

Sweet. Maybe that meant he could expect to get paid at some point.

She moved over to where four sturdy and spacious outdoor pens stood against a seen-better-days cattle fence.

"My brothers helped me build these." Maybe he'd read her wrong earlier, because now that she was in her element, she seemed relaxed. Pride shone on her face as she clipped a lead on a Portuguese water dog and led her out of the pen. "This is Tallulah. She's slated to be a diabetic service dog for an adorable five-year-old boy. She knows how to sit, stay and lay down."

"I like the idea of rescuing calm dogs to train. This will be different, because I usually work with puppies."

He hoped all his years of military training would help him win this battle for the job because his daughter seemed happy here. And lately, that was a rarity.

Anyway, Doc Earl had already told him that Autumn had been searching for months with no takers. Surely she'd give him a chance.

She crouched down to give Tallulah one last snuggle, then returned the mostly black dog with curly hair back to the pen.

"How many hours a week were you thinking?" he asked.

A puff of wind brushed a tumble of hair against her rosy cheek. "I'd like to say however long it takes. But being realistic, I'd say an hour or two most evenings and a full day on Saturday? Maybe a little on Sunday?"

He nodded. He could give her that time, and Harper would enjoy living on a farm.

They returned to the mouth of the dog barn and he spied Harper lying on the grass, Baby opposite her, sitting at attention. The terrier was adorable, mostly white with a few striking brown spots on her torso. His daughter's lips were moving, likely telling the dog one of her fanciful stories.

A warm breeze carried the scents of earth and cow over the rolling land, creating a peaceful feeling in his core. Man, he'd like to live on this ranch.

He glanced at the garage again. If he didn't get this apartment, where would they live? He and Harper couldn't stay with his mom and grandmother forever in that tiny two-bedroom apartment because Nana was undergoing intense chemotherapy. She didn't need a rambunctious four-year-old around, especially one with night terrors. No, Nana deserved uninterrupted sleep and quiet during these treatments, which meant he and Harper needed to move out. Soon.

When they had found out about Nana's cancer prognosis and his mother moved to Serenity to help, Wyatt decided to follow his mother because she was the only other adult Harper connected with. So when he discovered the vet tech position was available at Mighty Paws, it was like God had paved the way for all of them to move here.

But since Serenity, Texas, was a tiny town, there weren't many housing options and none were close to his budget. Living rent-free was his only chance to take control of his life and knock down the debt his drug addicted ex-wife had incurred on their joint credit cards. The debt he'd tried unsuccessfully to get out of in court.

"Autumn, I'd really like the job."

Something sharpened in her eyes. Maybe she was finally willing to give him a chance. "I've been working on basic obedience and socializing the dogs both here and in town. Unfortunately, more service dogs are released from training programs across the country for socialization concerns than for any other reason, so I wanted to get started on them right away."

Wow. She'd really thought this through. Her determination and drive intrigued him.

When she turned to him, the seriousness in her sparkling green eyes took him aback. "You probably think all this is silly."

"No. Not at all. You've got a nice operation here, and I'd love to be a part of it."

The hesitation in her attitude morphed into pride. "Thanks." The tentative smile she'd given Harper reappeared.

He recalled the captivating time they'd spent together at the resort. If he moved to the Triple C Ranch, would he and Autumn pick back up where they'd left off? He took a step back. No. Back then, he'd had a good reason not to get involved. Today, his reason was even stronger. He even had the divorce and wounded child to prove it.

"I've promised my client that Tallulah will be ready to go by July first, that's the dog-in-home deadline."

He reared back. "What? It usually takes six to twelve months to train a service dog."

"Yes, for puppies. But Tallulah is three-years-old, potty-trained and I've worked with her on obedience and socialization training. Anyway, Tanner needs her for summer camp or he can't go." The warmth in her eyes evaporated as she nailed him with a steely gaze. "Tanner has diabetes, and Tallulah will alert him when he has low blood sugar."

Before he could respond, she continued. "Camp is mid-July. I figured the boy would need the dog a few weeks early so they could bond and you could train Tanner as needed."

"That date is impossible."

She shrugged. "Then I'll keep looking."

Except, they both knew she had no other prospects. He

glanced at her parents' serene garage apartment, while Harper and Baby romped around like old friends on the crushed grass. This seemed like the perfect setting to build a life for himself and Harper. And look at her, she was happy here.

It was already the middle of April, so that gave him two and a half months to train a dog he hadn't yet evaluated. Nights and weekends only.

"Fine." He agreed. "I can't promise, but I'll try."

Even though he'd given in to her on what seemed like an insurmountable task, a look of unease washed over her features.

A glance at his watch proved it was already eight. He'd have to get going soon. He and Doc Earl had a nine-thirty surgery at the vet clinic and Wyatt still needed to drop his daughter at day care. But first he wanted to snag the job and apartment.

Harper raced over, the yipping terrier close behind. "Can we see my new bedroom now?"

Autumn gulped, but gave her a firm nod. "I guess so."

They climbed the steps on the side of the garage. The whole while his daughter talked about the *My Little Pony* decals her grandmother had found to decorate her new bedroom. It was the most he'd heard Harper utter at one time in months. The Triple C Ranch seemed to bring out a more confident side of her.

Autumn opened the aquamarine blue door and late morning sunshine streamed in through large windows overlooking a grove of trees. The generous living space was furnished, minus a couch.

"My sister-in-law is using the couch for her wedding venue, so whoever lives here will have to provide one," she said as she turned and waved her hand at the kitchen with an island. An island!

Harper raced to the back to check out her bedroom.

"It's only a one-bedroom, so clearly it won't work for you and your daughter." Her expression showed relief.

"It's actually perfect for us. She gets the room and I'll wake up to that serene view." He gestured at the floor-to-ceiling windows in the living room. The seven-foot couch he'd seen for sale yesterday at the consignment shop downtown would work for him, and it was on deep discount.

Harper raced back and threw her arms around Autumn's legs. "I love it, Miss Autumn. There's even a bench under the window where I can set up my dollies so they can watch the cows while I'm in day care."

Autumn seemed taken aback by Harper's quick affection and gave her an awkward pat on the back. At least Harper didn't notice her standoffish behavior. Maybe Autumn wasn't comfortable around kids.

Releasing her grasp on Autumn, his daughter raced to the island. "Look, an extra counter, just like Nana has."

Autumn turned to him, pulled a key from her pocket and handed it to him. "You can move in whenever works for you."

He shoved the key in his pocket as his gaze roamed their new cozy home.

What if he moved in, got Harper settled and then he and Autumn had a conflict that ended their agreement? Would he have to uproot his daughter all over again? No, that would be disastrous.

He prayed Autumn's personal feelings about him wouldn't make him lose this new home and Harper's chance at happiness.

Chapter Two

Later that afternoon, Harper perched below the bench under the window and played with her dolls while Wyatt leaned against the doorframe. He was thrilled his daughter appeared happy and content, because an hour ago, things were wildly different.

Yesterday had been his first day working for Doc Earl. The day care had called after an hour, and the sweet veterinarian had allowed Harper to color in the waiting room for the rest of the day. But a business was no place for a four-year-old, and unfortunately his mother was knee-deep in caring for his grandmother.

So today, when he'd received a call midday to pick her up again, Doc Earl had given him the afternoon off, telling him the schedule was light today. His boss had acted supportive and insisted Harper just needed a little time to adjust. But Wyatt was concerned about his job. He couldn't keep working partial days and expect full pay. At some point, Doc Earl would lose patience, and Wyatt needed this job.

He strode down the small hallway and through the open door of the apartment. At least they had time to move in before darkness fell. The more time Harper had to adjust, he figured the better chance she'd sleep well tonight.

He dashed down the steps and hastily pulled more of the packed boxes out of his truck bed.

"I thought you were working today?" Autumn asked from the dog barn with Baby cradled in her arms.

He looked up and smiled, well tried to. Earlier in the day, when Autumn had spotted him for the first time, she had gone white and her mouth had dropped open in surprise. He knew how she felt. He'd been just as shocked to see her after all this time. Except he couldn't figure out why she was as prickly as a porcupine about them working together. She needed a dog trainer. He needed an apartment. It didn't seem that complicated to him.

As she walked down the incline, he balanced the boxes in his arms. "Knocked off a little early so we could move in before dinner."

"Good. That means you can start the dog training today," she snapped. Baby swiped a tongue over her chin, and Autumn pressed the dog closer to her chest. The terrier sure acted like an emotional support dog. "Do you want to start with Winston or Tallulah?"

He climbed the steps, juggling the boxes with an impatient Autumn on his heels. "Let me move in and settle my daughter. If I have time left over—"

"That wasn't the agreement," she retorted.

"Daddy," Harper cried, and then appeared on the landing. "Where were you?" Worry covered her sweet face.

"Right here, sweetheart." He rushed up the remaining steps, set the boxes to the side and engulfed her in a hug.

Ever since the last visit with her mother, Harper had experienced night terrors and was unusually clingy, even during the day. But that was before the move to Serenity. He hoped she'd moved on from the issues now that Chloe was in jail and Harper didn't have to worry about seeing her mother anymore.

"Why are you holding Baby upside down, Miss Autumn?" The sight of their landlord and her dog brightened Harper's demeanor as she pushed away from him and cocked her head.

Autumn dropped to her knees and set Baby on the landing. "Just snuggling."

Harper giggled. "Want to see my new bedroom?"

"Of course," Autumn said with a tentative smile, and he watched as the two tromped into the apartment. "She is so adorable." His new boss threw over her shoulder as the duo headed down the hall.

Her long blond hair bounced as she walked. She was even more gorgeous than he remembered from their time on the island. His eyes had caught on a faint smattering of freckles across the bridge of her pert nose when she'd smiled at Harper.

Small puffy clouds captured his attention as they dotted an otherwise blue sky. The peacefulness of the surroundings settled deep within, creating a longing Wyatt hadn't felt in a while. But Autumn didn't seem pleased to have him here, so he shouldn't get too comfortable. He gathered the boxes and moved inside as Autumn sauntered back to the kitchen.

"Can I help?" she asked, then scooted to the side as he carried the boxes into the kitchen and set them on the counter.

Wyatt silently prayed that his relationship with Autumn would smooth out and he'd be able to keep this apartment. Four years ago he'd become a believer. But when his wife had descended into prescription drug dependency, he'd needed God even more.

"I've got it," he answered, then spotted the lost look in her emerald eyes right as the gentle breeze lifted her fragrance and wrapped the sweet smell around the kitchen.

The last thing he wanted was for her to feel unwelcome. Especially after she'd taken a chance on hiring him. "You can help as soon as I figure out what's in these." He chuckled and waved at the stack on the counter.

Hesitating, she stepped forward. "Wow, that couch is long."

He eyed the seven-foot velvet green couch her brother had just helped him move in. "I needed somewhere to sleep, and this perfect piece was at the consignment shop downtown at a deep discount."

She ran her fingertips along the back. "Nice."

He reached into a packing box, took out his meager cookie sheets and slid them into the drawer under the range. "So why service dogs? Why not train emotional support dogs?" Because it seemed she had trained Baby. And she wouldn't need a trainer if she was matching people with ES dogs.

"I went to some intensive training classes with Baby because I wanted to take her to the children's hospital and put a smile on kids' faces." She turned to him, her features suddenly closed off. "While at the training, I learned the difference between ESAs and service dogs and it struck a chord. So many people, children especially, need scent-based animals to help them safely get through their days."

Her gaze flitted away before she continued. "Baby is a rescue dog. Years ago, I worked at a shelter and she came in. I just knew she was for me." Her chin lifted in defiance, as though she were waiting for him to tell her that her business was a stupid idea. He would do no such thing because he thought it was genius. "Anyway, I have a thing for rescued animals, so I decided to rescue adult dogs that were under three or four and had a calm personality to train."

"I like that you're rescuing dogs to train. Giving the dog a new home and purpose."

"I've always felt strongly about rescuing versus buying puppies."

His admiration level inched up a notch at her desire to train rescue dogs and match them with people in need.

Their gazes locked and the passion he saw in the depths of her emerald green irises caused his pulse to jump.

Whoa. This was only a work relationship, nothing more. He took a step back. Chloe had taught him the hard way not to trust.

Harper rushed into the kitchen, breaking the moment, Baby barking at her heels. "Can we go see the other dogs now, please?"

Autumn laughed at Harper's quiet plea and said they absolutely could.

When his daughter's hand slipped into hers, Autumn's eyes widened in surprise. She quickly recovered and seemed to give Harper her full attention as they walked down the steps.

He prayed the move to Serenity was exactly what his daughter needed to put the past behind her and become the confident little girl Wyatt knew she could be.

At the base of the steps, Harper released Autumn's hand and raced after Baby. Autumn stopped and aimed a weak smile at his little girl.

"She's such a happy child," she said. Her interactions with his daughter seemed unsure, even awkward. Clearly, Autumn wasn't used to being around young children.

He breathed in the fresh country air. Harper seemed so

free right now. Not trapped in scary memories from the difficult times with her mother.

A couple of horses neighed in a paddock nearby. Across the way, Angus cattle were munching on grass.

"Let's get started training."

A quick glance at his watch proved it was nearly dinnertime. "I planned on feeding Harper some dinner and having a quiet evening to get her settled in."

"She looks occupied right now."

Well, he only had the apartment because Autumn expected him to train Tallulah in a crazy short amount of time, so he relented. "Okay, I have the raised platform in the bed of my truck. Let me get it."

"Wait. I've already trained them on basic obedience. You just need to add the scent detection."

"Listen, Autumn, while in the military, I was always working on developing my skills. I took side programs and taught courses to help civilians." That was where he'd learned about platform training. "If we're going to work with rescues who haven't been trained since birth as a working dog, we need to make them realize they are in working mode. The best way to train them is on a climb platform. We'll get to scent detection in time."

She flashed an irritated look at him. "Look, I've researched how to train scent detection dogs. I didn't see any requirements for using a platform. It frankly sounds like a waste of time to me."

"Autumn, training service dogs is a process. I first need to build a relationship with the dog. Then work with them using my command words, so I kind of need to start at the beginning, though the basic obedience should go quickly since you've already worked with Tallulah."

She pursed her lips together as he headed to his truck

for the platform. He glimpsed Harper playing with Baby as though she didn't have a care in the world. The sight of his daughter carefree lifted his heart.

But if Autumn was going to question his training skills before he even started, their working relationship might fail. Trepidation swirled in his gut.

What had happened to the fun-loving Autumn he'd spent that glorious day with at the resort? The amazing woman he hadn't been able to forget. Perhaps his memories of their time together were fonder than hers were. That would explain her odd behavior toward him.

Cows mooing in the distance brought him out of his musings.

All he wanted was for his little girl to forget the past and enjoy her childhood. And the Triple C Ranch appeared to soothe her like he hadn't seen in a while.

Which meant he had to prove to Autumn that he was the best trainer for the job so they could stay.

Autumn opened Winston's pen, snapped the leash on his harness and joined Wyatt behind the dog barn. He motioned to the platform in his arms and asked where she wanted it. She pointed to the space next to the third pen, and he tipped it on two legs there.

"I'd prefer to build a relationship with the dogs first," he said. "It would make the initial training go much faster."

"Let's just jump in. These dogs are pretty advanced." There was no way she'd stand for him to spend days on end *building a relationship* with them. She had a timetable to keep. It was bad enough he insisted on starting the dogs over on obedience training.

"Who's this?" Wyatt cocked his head at the golden retriever.

"Winston. He's slated to be a diabetic service dog for a single adult who lives alone." She brought the golden retriever over. For now, she had to follow Wyatt's rules because she wanted to meet her client's promised deadlines, and without him, she would fail.

"Tallulah is our priority," he snapped. "Remember the July date we discussed?"

"I remember, but I wanted you to meet Winston. Maybe start the training with him."

"But—"

She narrowed her eyes at him. "Humor me."

After a moment he said, "you're the boss."

"Let me get him a service vest," Wyatt said, as he shrugged out of a large black backpack that must have come from his truck as well. He fished out a large red vest and replaced the golden retriever's harness.

Was it her imagination, or was Winston standing taller with that official vest on?

She had to give Wyatt credit. Not only was he accredited through the Air Force, but he'd furthered his training by taking outside classes and taught civilians as well. Very ambitious. One of the things that had attracted her to him at the resort.

But they weren't at the resort anymore. Autumn sure hoped she and Wyatt could find a rhythm to their working relationship and end up being a successful team, because she already felt like a failure for not making something of herself, like her siblings had. They all had a focus in life and her parents were so proud of each of them. She wanted that for herself.

Wyatt set the backpack on a hay bale leaning against the dog barn and slipped on a paper-thin nylon vest with bulging pockets. His features were more rugged, making him appear even more handsome than years ago.

Did he know what he was doing? He was used to training German shepherd puppies, not older rescue dogs. Maybe she shouldn't have been so quick to let him move into the apartment?

Except she'd spoken with every dog trainer in a sixty-mile radius, and not one of them would even consider her position because it was unpaid. So what choice did she have but to hire Wyatt?

Anyway, she felt bad for Harper since she was motherless. Autumn could tell right away that the little girl was shy around strangers and new places. But this morning, once she'd met Baby, she'd come out of her shell pretty quickly. Autumn just wished the girl hadn't glommed onto her so fast. Harper's attachment to Autumn only added to the complications she already felt toward Wyatt for not answering her calls seven years ago.

Anyway, with him around, she might be forced to work through the painful emotions she'd kept stuffed deep inside. Her stomach tilted at the notion.

Lord, help me handle all the unwanted feelings about the past that are hurtling into my head. She paused and wondered if He would hear her.

Sure, she had a sturdy relationship with the Lord, but it was predicated on her solid belief that God was punishing her for her past.

"What was your release command?"

She startled at Wyatt's voice. "All done."

He nodded and turned to Winston, then put the dog in a down stay position and released him with the command *free*.

Now why did it matter what term was used to release the

dog? Frustration at the man grew. Maybe she should have taken classes and gotten a training certificate herself. Of course, it would have taken a year, and she'd have missed her first three dog-in-home deadlines. She scrunched up her nose and sighed. No, a certified trainer was the best option.

Every time Wyatt released Winston in his firm, clear voice, he gave the golden retriever a small treat from his pocket vest. The dog learned the new release term easily, which made Autumn feel like she'd done something right training the handsome golden.

Wyatt lowered the platform, covered in a blanket of artificial grass. Winston immediately hopped on top, wandered the area and sniffed. The moment he jumped down, Wyatt said *free* and shoved a treat at Winston. So the dog cocked his head and then did a sit stay in front of the trainer, then tried a down stay. When no treats came, he hopped onto the platform, keeping an eye on the trainer, then jumped off. Wyatt repeated the *free* command and gave him another treat. It took a few times, but Winston figured out that jumping onto the platform and then hopping off made Wyatt give the release command and the treat. The whole time, Wyatt stayed close to Winston so he could immediately treat the dog.

Autumn was taken aback by how quickly Winston was learning and how focused the dog was on Wyatt.

Maybe she had made the right hiring decision. Then memories flooded her head, reminding her that Wyatt was the last person she wanted to work with.

"You know, I never thought about training an older dog or a rescue into a service animal," he said.

She felt puffed up by the indirect praise. "Even though they might learn slower than younger dogs or need to unlearn some habits, distractions might be easier for them to overcome."

"You've done your homework and picked a good one in Winston." He slid her a sideways smile, reminding her of their time together on the island and how charming he was.

Which was why she couldn't get over that he'd ignored her calls and texts. Why? They'd gotten along fabulously. Had he ghosted her because he was afraid she wanted a relationship?

He shoved his hands into his jeans pockets, drawing her attention. A black T-shirt stretched across his muscular chest. She could kick herself for not being more explicit with the voicemails she'd left. She hadn't wanted to tell him the exact reason in a message, so she'd been vague.

"Harper seems to love it here. *Free*," he said. Every time he uttered the release word, he held out a treat that Winston gobbled up. "She's had some difficulties in the past, *free*, and I just want the best for her. This ranch seems to calm her, *free*, so thank you."

His concerns were loving and thoughtful. Harper might only have one involved parent, but he was doing an admirable job.

Autumn's heart sighed at how much he clearly loved Harper. He seemed like a great guy, so why had he reacted with silence years ago?

"Daddy!" Harper shrieked as she rushed over and grabbed his leg. The penned dogs started barking, but Winston sat stock-still and waited for Wyatt to give his attention to the dog. Wyatt crouched down and enveloped his daughter in a fierce bear hug. His love and concern radiated through the space.

Autumn shook her head. No matter how uncomfortable she was with him here, there was no way she would consider getting rid of Wyatt now that she knew Harper had a difficult past and was happy here. The last thing Autumn would do was hurt the little girl.

Harper squirmed out of his embrace. He asked if she was having a good time on the ranch, and she replied yes. Then he roughed up her hair. The sweet gesture made Autumn smile. He was a doting father. Harper grinned and took off after Baby again.

"I think we're done for the day. Tomorrow we'll introduce the container," he said as he exchanged Winston's service vest for his harness. "You've done good work with this dog. I like it."

Autumn soaked in the compliment like a parched field on a rainy day. She wanted to stay mad at him, but if he kept exhibiting such kindness, it would be hard.

"So, do you think we can meet the August first date for him?" she asked.

"What?" Wyatt balked. "You promised Tallulah for July. That gives me two and a half months to prepare her, which I already told you is a stretch. And now Winston, only a short month later?"

She pursed her lips and tried to hide her annoyance that he disagreed with her deadlines.

"How did you come up with these dates when you didn't even have a trainer?"

She studied his face and decided he deserved to know how she'd gotten herself into this unfortunate bind.

"Walt, Winston's owner, kind of gave me the date he needed the dog trained by. And since Tanner's camp starts in the middle of July, I figured he would need some time with Tallulah before camp started."

Wyatt just stared at her, and his jaw shifted, as though

entirely displeased with her. As he probably should be. Her need to please had put him in a difficult position.

Her gaze found the ground. "When I started the business, I thought I could train the dogs on my own since there are so many videos online that I could mimic. Then, after I started, I kind of got in over my head."

He nodded, accepting her explanation, which she was thankful for. "I get you don't want to disappoint Walt and Tanner, but the time frame is very tight. I've never seen dogs trained that quickly." The concern in his eyes proved he'd never made that tight of a deadline before.

She pushed her worry away because she'd made a promise, and she kept her promises. She waited to see if he'd agree.

Wyatt rubbed a hand over his buzz cut, the hair popping back into place. "I'll try to hit the dog-in-home dates you've promised, but if either of the dogs doesn't get it right away, we'll have to speak with your clients and modify the schedule, okay? Because my reputation is on the line."

"Mine too." She nodded, thrilled he was being so understanding. "But I know Tallulah and Winston will pick up the training right away. They are both super smart."

Wyatt sighed. "Okay. And don't forget that Tanner's mother needs to collect his saliva sample on clean dental cotton when his blood sugar level is low and freeze it for us to use for training."

Her spirits lifted at his positive response. "So we can do it?"

He glared at her. "I'll try, but I don't have confidence that we'll meet either of your aggressive promised dates."

Her heart sank at his pessimism.

What would she do if they didn't hit the deadlines she

had promised her clients? Her business might fail before it got off the ground.

Heavyhearted, she returned Winston to his pen.

Failure was not an option, but at this moment she had no control over the training schedule. Somehow she'd have to trust that Wyatt would put in the work necessary to get Tallulah and Winston to their forever homes on their allotted dates.

That implied she had to figure out a way to trust Wyatt, even though an enormous secret lay between them. With no other options, she had been forced to hire him, and now he would be around all the time.

Which meant the memories of the emotionally painful miscarriage that she'd so painstakingly hidden in her past would haunt her daily.

At some point, she'd probably feel obligated to tell him what had happened. And if she told him, it'd open up the wound she'd so carefully buried away. Like a loose thread on a sweater, once she told him the secret, and he deserved to know even though he had answered none of her calls, it might leak out to her loved ones and create even more distance between them.

She squeezed her eyes shut. Her life was unraveling quicker than a group of excited cows using their noses to unroll a giant hay bale, and she didn't know how to halt the progression.

Chapter Three

Of course, she'd be stuck alone in an exam room with Wyatt. Autumn should have thought about that before coming in for Winston's vaccine appointment. Seemed being around Wyatt was causing past memories to claw at her, just like she feared would happen. Memories she'd successfully squashed for years. She should have brought Baby for emotional support. What had she been thinking, leaving her terrier at home?

To get her mind off Wyatt, she studied the pet murals that made each exam room unique, but the walls felt like they were closing in on her. She fanned herself, but lowered her hand as soon as he looked her way.

Every time he gave her that adorable crooked smile, he reminded her of their brief time together and the aftermath. She gritted her teeth. After the past four days at the Triple C, she should be used to being around him, but she wasn't. Somehow she'd have to learn how to survive being in the same room as the man who had ignored her calls and text messages when she had needed him.

After taking Winston's vital signs, Wyatt recorded them on the clipboard. "Doc Earl should be in momentarily," he said. His voice held a buoyancy that she absolutely didn't feel.

With his good looks, charismatic personality and strict

work ethic, the women of Serenity were no doubt doing everything they could to snag a date with him.

Not that she was interested. At all. She'd learned her lesson.

She stepped closer to the wall, putting some space between them and wishing again that she had Baby to hold close.

Wyatt and his daughter had even attended church with the McCaws on Sunday and sat in their family's pew. But thankfully hadn't come to lunch at the main house afterward. There was only so much of Wyatt and her secret that she could handle, and working with him and the dogs was pushing it.

He'd spent a good bit of time over the weekend with Tallulah and Winston, and Autumn was feeling very confident with her promised dates, even if he wasn't.

"So, there's this festival coming up over Memorial Day weekend." She nibbled her lip. Would he think she was crazy to take part in an arts and crafts gathering? In her defense, lots of nonartsy businesses participated. Why was she even bringing up the festival? He'd rejected her in the past, so he'd likely insult her marketing as well.

He turned, as if surprised she was being nice to him because she'd kind of snapped at him all weekend. She really needed to rein in her hostility. Maybe he had a good reason for ignoring her previously. If she had the guts to ask, she could get it all out in the open. But it seemed easier to let sleeping dogs lie.

"A festival?" he asked.

"It'll be an opportunity to teach the community about my dog boarding, and now that you're training, I can advertise about the service dog element as well."

"Sounds good."

"I was hoping you could help." At his surprised look, she hurried through the spiel she'd been practicing in her head. "Maybe show off some training skills?"

"Sure, glad to," he answered immediately. "I know how important it is to you to place trained pups with people. And who knows, sounds like there might be food there. I love me a tasty festival corn dog."

She gave a little clap, then averted her eyes as she remembered who she was talking to. "If you help me, I'll buy you all the corn dogs you can eat."

"Will you have a booth?" When she gazed up into his enticing chocolate eyes, she had to look away real quick. Wyatt showing up after all this time, right when her life was finally on track, had her on edge. She so wanted to sit in her self-righteous anger, but sometimes he was so nice to her that he made it hard.

"Yes." She informed him of all the specifics, and he didn't even laugh when she told him it was technically an arts and crafts festival. Maybe she had him pegged wrong. Perhaps working together wouldn't be as challenging as she had once thought.

"Maybe we can use Tallulah," she said, "but I'm not sure she's big enough. Do you think everyone could see her? We could use Winston since he's a golden retriever." She encircled her arms around the dog's neck and nuzzled into his fur to keep from rambling any more than she already had.

"Let's use Tallulah. She's the furthest along and she isn't that small. She's a good thirty pounds."

Wyatt was being so kind and thoughtful. She felt bad about avoiding him. But maybe he hadn't noticed she wasn't keen having him work for her.

His phone buzzed, and he held up a *just a moment* finger. When he looked at the display, his face fell. "It's the day care."

He answered, then listened intently. After a moment, he became distressed. "I'll be right over," he said, then hung up.

When his shoulders dropped and he looked off in the distance, Autumn's heart ached for him. Whatever his daughter was going through was not only difficult on her, but on him as well. She wanted to reach out and pat his arm, tell him it would be okay, but she wouldn't dare do that. First off, she didn't want to overstep and get into his personal space, since they were no longer close. Second off, she didn't know if things would be okay with Harper. She wasn't a parent. She had no idea what his darling daughter was going through.

"I don't know what I'm going to do," he said. "Though Doc Earl loves Harper, this is a business. And we have surgeries today in about an hour." His lips turned down as he appeared deep in thought. "I wish I could somehow help Harper get over her fears and anxiety," he whispered.

Tears sprang to Autumn's eyes at his genuine love toward his daughter. "I'm so sorry she's going through all this."

Emotions flitted over his face before he schooled his features. "My ex-wife put me through the wringer." His voice shook with regret. "Unfortunately, the ramifications of that relationship still haunt Harper to this day."

Oh, Harper. It hurt Autumn's heart to hear that his daughter's struggles were related to her mother. Your parents should be the two people in the world who had your back. But apparently Harper's mother had issues that were leaking into the little girl's life. Maybe Wyatt had ignored Autumn's calls and texts, but his life had not been easy since they parted. Not by a long shot.

"I've been praying for her to not only adjust to her new

day care situation," she said, "but to heal from whatever... trauma she's been going through."

"Thank you, Autumn, you're right. I just have to keep praying and loving." He exhaled a deep breath and glanced at his watch. "Okay, I guess I need to let Doc Earl know I have to leave."

Autumn could almost hear Wyatt's internal warring to keep his word to Earl and somehow support his adorable daughter at the same time.

As Wyatt reached for the doorknob, her eyes widened at his predicament. If Wyatt lost his job here, she'd lose him as a dog trainer. She sucked in a breath. "Wait."

He turned, and she licked her lips. Should she offer, or would it be too emotionally challenging?

"I'll pick up Harper from day care for you." She spoke before she could think it through. She shrugged like it was no big deal, but this was humongous. Though she didn't have a choice because Wyatt needed to stay employed so he could train her dogs. Period. She'd do everything in her power to help him stay on Earl's good side, which shouldn't be too difficult since the local veterinarian was a teddy bear.

"Are you sure?" When shock covered his face, she tried not to take it personally. He was probably just surprised that a virtual stranger was offering to help. And it's not as though she'd felt comfortable with Harper since they arrived, but maybe he hadn't noticed.

No doubt he was thinking she couldn't handle watching his active daughter for a few hours.

A niggle of doubt wound around her core. She knew nothing about parenting or kids.

She shook off the negativity. The most important thing was he needed to remain in Serenity. Employed.

"I was going back to the ranch anyway," she stated, as though watching a kid was no big deal. "Harper can just hang out with me."

She refused to take the indecision on his face personally. Wyatt's strained smile told her that while he appreciated her offer, he also hated not being able to do it himself. Maybe accepting help wasn't something that came naturally to him.

Before Wyatt got out the door, Earl came in and gave Winston his shots, then scooted out because of the busy morning. Without her asking, Wyatt moved the golden to the ground for her.

Be still my heart. He was a Southern gentleman after all. She pushed the kind appraisal away because years ago, the man had hurt her and she couldn't forget the pain.

After profusely thanking her, Wyatt accompanied her to the parking lot so he could move Harper's booster seat into Autumn's well-used SUV coated in dog hair, while Autumn put Winston in his crate in the back.

He then called the day care to give Autumn a onetime permission to pick up Harper.

"Thanks again, Autumn. I really appreciate this," he said, then he put his hand on her shoulder for a moment.

The warmth from his hand radiated into her skin and piqued her interest in the man.

Stop. He meant nothing by the brief touch.

After they parted, she got behind the wheel and pointed her vehicle toward the day care center and waited for her racing heartbeat to slow.

The trees and shrubs became misty as she stared out through the windshield as she traveled across town, and the gravity of what she'd offered to do washed over her.

Her heart jumped in her throat at being responsible for

another human being, even if only for a few hours. Could she really take care of busy Harper all by herself?

Ever since she'd met the little girl, Autumn had been dwelling on the baby she never had.

She pulled into the day care parking lot. She had no choice. Even though Wyatt was the last person she wanted to work with, he was her only option. And he needed to stay employed at Mighty Paws Veterinarian Clinic to keep helping Autumn.

Somehow, she'd get through the afternoon. She had no alternative if she wanted Wyatt to keep his job.

As soon as work ended, Wyatt rushed to the Triple C and slammed his truck into Park. He touched the door handle to exit but looked up and froze at the sight.

In the field between her parents' house and the dog barn, Autumn waved a huge wand back and forth, creating gigantic bubbles. Harper, pure joy on her face, pressed her hands forward as though she were swimming through the bubble.

He released a nervous sigh. His baby was just fine.

While he studied Autumn through the bug-splattered windshield, he scrubbed a hand over his face. He'd learned early in his marriage not to rely on others because they'd just let him down. When his wife chose pain management drugs over him and their newborn child, he'd lost trust in her. When she'd chosen other men, he'd lost faith in their marriage.

Now he questioned what God was doing here. With Autumn. And with forcing Wyatt to lean on others, something he found downright uncomfortable.

He rubbed the back of his neck and let out a deep, frustrated sigh. *Lord, are you going to tell me what's going on, or am I going to have to figure it out on my own?*

Silence.

Tomorrow morning, he'd spend some quiet time with God and maybe figure all this confusing stuff out.

He exited the car, thrilled to see a smile on Harper's face. After the emergency call he'd gotten from day care a few hours ago, her sunny mood warmed his heart. He had half expected Autumn to place a frantic call to him, but the afternoon had been quiet and productive.

He strode over to the playful pair, reluctant to rely on someone new. His mother had moved in with them after the car accident that had left Chloe, and newborn Harper, in the hospital. She'd been his extra set of hands for the past four trying years, so accepting help from Autumn was not in his comfort zone.

"Daddy," Harper screamed and rushed to him. His worries disappeared as he lifted her and flew her in a circle like an airplane. The grin on her face, oh my, he hadn't seen that in a while. And it was all because of Autumn and her kindness.

Though he'd accomplished building a life for himself and his daughter since arriving in Serenity, he hadn't done it alone. He relied on Autumn for his home, and this afternoon she'd made a tight connection with Harper.

"Thank you," he said to Autumn with a nod as he put his daughter on the ground.

"Anytime."

No. This was a onetime thing and his reliance on Autumn stopped now.

It was one thing to rely on family. His mother wasn't going anywhere. But he needed to be cautious about letting Autumn into their life.

Yes, his mother was focused on helping his grandmother through her treatments and he no longer felt able to reach out to her as much, but he should have at least tried. Both he and Doc Earl had been working against the clock today to get all their patients seen and perform the scheduled surgeries, so Autumn's offer had been the easiest solution. But as a parent, easy wasn't always the smartest choice.

Autumn waved another bubble into being. Harper chased it down and then rushed over to Autumn for a hug.

Wyatt's shoulders tensed. His goal had been to create a new life for him and his daughter, not have his daughter trust another woman who would surely let her down.

What would happen when Autumn was no longer in their life? Harper struggled when she lost people she cared about, and Wyatt wanted to shield his little girl from any more pain.

"More, more," Harper called, clapping her hands.

"Okay, Bug." Autumn swished the wand in the soapy water and waved more bubbles into the air.

His heart hiccupped at the sweet term his Nana used for Harper. What had prompted Autumn to use it?

He drew in a breath at his combined frustration and gratefulness toward her. Maybe he was being too harsh, because she clearly cared for Harper. The watery smile Autumn gave his daughter wormed into his heart and reminded him of the fun times they had at the resort. Autumn was a sweet woman. Attractive. Funny. Loyal.

His daughter brought out a softer side in Autumn, one he found quite attractive. He pushed away the undesirable thoughts, reminding himself how messy relationships could become.

Harper squealed as she jumped through a double bubble, and Autumn's low laugh sucked him in, stirring up memories from the past.

"Well, I appreciate you watching Harper for me," he

said. "I'm sure it was an inconvenience. I'll make other plans in the future."

"I was happy to watch her. She's fun," Autumn said, focused solely on Harper. Had she even looked him in the eye since he arrived this afternoon? He had been so focused on his own issues, he'd forgotten she'd been acting icy toward him.

When they'd parted ways seven years ago, she'd told him she'd just gotten out of a painful relationship and wasn't interested in anything long term. So what was causing her to treat him like a pariah since they'd reconnected?

It didn't matter. He and Autumn didn't have to get along for him to train dogs and live here rent free. In fact, it'd be better if they kept it all business. Cleaner for when he and Harper were ready to move on.

"Horsey," Harper stated and rushed over to the animal.

"Stay on this side of the fence," he called and was rewarded with a glare over the shoulder.

Autumn busied herself putting away the bubbles, then stacking them with a slew of other toys, mostly still shrink-wrapped.

"Did you purchase all that?" He pointed to the pile of toys.

Her cheeks pinked. "After I picked up Harper, we dropped Winston off and then returned to the toy store real quick because the forecast called for rain. I thought bracelet making would be fun." She wrinkled her nose.

His ex-wife had impulsively spent too, and mistakenly believed spending money would make her, and those around her, happy. He shrugged away the unwelcome memory, thankful that Autumn had not only taken care of Harper this afternoon, but had put thought into their activities.

"How'd the surgeries go?" Autumn asked as Baby trotted over. She scooped the dog into her arms and nuzzled her fur.

"There were four, and they were all textbook. Thanks for asking." He loved his job at the vet clinic. When he realized he'd have to separate from the military, he'd been concerned about civilian life, especially a career. But Mighty Paws and Doc Earl were an answered prayer. And frankly, working for Autumn scratched the itch he'd probably always have—training dogs.

But no matter how nice Doc Earl was, he wouldn't keep paying Wyatt if he continued leaving early to pick up his daughter. Doc Earl had already implied that having Harper in the office unattended was an insurance liability.

Harper rushed back and slipped her palm into Autumn's free hand.

"Thank Miss Autumn, sweetheart. We need to have dinner and let Autumn get back to work."

"Miss Autumn, can you have dinner with us?" Harper asked.

He held in his exasperated sigh. How had she gotten so attached to Autumn so quickly? He'd had a long day, and he just wanted a simple dinner of boxed macaroni and cheese with his daughter before his dog training began.

Autumn's cheeks flushed while she looked between father and daughter. She was gorgeous, not to mention smart and career focused. When she shook her head, her mane of unruly caramel-colored hair tumbled over her shoulders in long waves.

He needed to stop encouraging these two from spending any more time together than was absolutely necessary.

Baby shifted her position so she could snuggle her head under her owner's chin. Autumn gazed into Baby's eyes, pressed a kiss on the terrier's forehead, right between the dog's eyes and then flicked a chilly glance at him before he could come up with an excuse to renege on his daughter's offer. "Maybe another time, Bug," she said as she crouched low to hug Harper. "I loved playing with you," she whispered, but Wyatt heard her. "Maybe we can do it again soon."

Her velvety voice, encouraging and affectionate, curled through his chest. He had a hard time pushing someone away who clearly adored Harper and looked as pretty as Autumn did while doing it.

"No, have dinner with us." Harper pouted.

"I'm sorry, Bug, but I need to get back to Winston and Tallulah. They need me."

Harper nodded. "Give them each a hug from me, okay?"

When Harper slipped her fingers in Wyatt's hand, Autumn turned, still clinging to Baby, and rushed away as if upset about something.

Why did his presence irritate Autumn? When they were discussing her training business, they had productive dialogues. But take dogs and training out of the conversation and something was off between them.

There was some type of underlying unease between them, but he had no idea what it was. The fixer in him wanted to know so he could mend the problem and give them a clean slate.

As he and Harper climbed the steps to their quaint apartment, a niggling conviction that he would be a more successful dog trainer if he and Autumn worked as a team rather than two individuals settled into his chest.

Earlier at the vet office, when she was talking up the festival, he got the impression it would generate more clients. The more clients she had, the more money she made. If she became profitable enough, she could afford a dog trainer's salary instead of offering free rent.

He opened their door and Harper rushed in to check on each of the dolls she had lined up on the couch earlier in the day.

If given the chance, would Autumn hire a different dog trainer?

Based on how annoyed he seemed to make her, he'd guess yes.

So then, maybe he should try to right whatever wrong was happening between them because he wanted to keep training dogs for Autumn. It was fun.

Anyway, he and Harper enjoyed living at the Triple C Ranch. He wasn't sure what would happen if they lost this little apartment.

Chapter Four

Wyatt pulled up the last rotted board, threw it over the edge of the landing to his little apartment, then wiped his brow. Only the middle of April and the beating sun was already scorching, but that was Texas for you. He leaned back and breathed in the comforting aromas of cows and hay. Harper had been flourishing since they moved in a week ago, and for that he was grateful.

He smiled at this little landing and the apartment that lay beyond. His daughter loved it here and fixing the rotted boards on this deck would make it their perfect home.

A vehicle caught his attention as it approached the Triple C. Autumn and her dusty SUV. He felt the hum of attraction at her arrival and attempted to disregard the unwelcome feelings by gathering some nails. He was still reeling from his ex-wife's multiple deceptions and the fallout Harper was living through from her mother. No, he couldn't have tender feelings toward Autumn. He'd been there, done that and wanted no part of a romantic relationship again.

Anyway, she'd been giving him the cold shoulder, and he had no idea why.

Autumn hopped out of the vehicle and stared up at him. Without thinking, he wiggled his fingers at her.

She frowned at him and then turned her attention to

her phone as Baby raced over to her and danced around in circles for attention.

Why did his mere existence seem to irritate Autumn? He shook off thoughts of the attractive woman and eyed the space, making a plan for how to lay the fresh boards on the landing. Maybe he should ask her why he annoyed her so.

Even though he didn't want to, he knew the best thing he could do for Harper was have a solid relationship with his landlord, and he'd do anything for his daughter. He hammered nails home to secure the first board.

Something was off with Autumn, but how was he supposed to have an open and honest conversation when she was snubbing him?

Footsteps sounded on the stairs. He peered down and spied Autumn on the steps, lifting each foot as if it were in quicksand. Baby was nestled in her arms like a...baby. He put his hammer down as she perched a few steps away from him and lifted her chin. She was a much different person now than when they'd met years ago.

She appeared so put together on the outside, but there seemed to be a ton of pain just beneath the surface and he wondered what it could be. He could probably spot it because he was the same. "What's up?" he asked.

"I was going to ask you the same thing. Lumber?" She focused on the landing and the open gaps where the rotted boards had been. She seemed unwilling to meet his gaze, like every other interaction from the past week.

Her long lashes brushed the tops of her pink cheeks. When she glanced back at him, he got caught in her sparkling eyes.

"Landing was rickety," he said, aiming his attention on the wood and not her appeal. "Don't want anyone to get hurt." With Harper out of earshot, now was the perfect time to broach her iciness toward him. "Laney's watching Harper so I can knock this out." He glanced at the little gingerbread house where Autumn's brother, Ethan, and his wife, Laney, lived with their three children. Did he have the nerve to ask her?

Autumn stared across the way toward Henry Wright's structure, her dog barn, as though making eye contact with him was unbearable, almost painful, for her. He racked his brain but couldn't think of what he had done to upset her so.

"This shouldn't take too long and then it'll be as good as new." He took in his apartment's aquamarine blue door. Since they moved in, Harper had been so happy and content. He wasn't sure if it was the fresh country air or the property or the friendly people or what, but he needed to fix whatever was bothering Autumn because he didn't want to lose their housing.

"I was thinking about the festival in May," she said, "maybe we could announce some basic obedience classes you could teach. Like an hour long on Saturdays or something."

"Seriously?" He frowned. He had more than enough on his plate without adding one more thing.

"Yes. I'll do all the paperwork. It's only one hour of your week and it'd build my business."

Slowly, he counted to ten. Somehow they had to work as a team. It was the only way for her business to succeed and for him to keep his apartment.

"Listen, Autumn, I have a full-time job, a daughter to raise and three dogs to train for special use. Though the group obedience class sounds like a good idea, I just don't have the time to devote to it."

She sulked and concentrated on the wooden steps under her feet. "Sure, I understand."

At that moment, she glanced up and caught his gaze, then looked away. He grimaced. What had he done to dismay her so? He reached out and touched her elbow. She flinched like he'd been about to hurt her. Baby licked Autumn's chin real quick, then gave him the stink eye.

"Autumn, what's going on?" He tried to make his voice as gentle as possible. He truly wanted to know why there was a huge brick wall between them when they'd gotten along so fabulously at the resort. "You're avoiding looking at me. Have I done something to offend you?"

"Everything is fine," she spat out. Baby wiggled higher and rested her snout on Autumn's shoulder.

No. Everything was not fine. He held in an exasperated breath.

"Well, you're nice to everyone yet short with me," he said. "Are you mad at me?"

"No, Wyatt, I'm not mad at you." But her chin wobbled, so he knew she wasn't being fully truthful.

He ran through their interactions since he arrived in Serenity, and nothing came to mind. Something must have happened in the past, yet their time on the island had been pretty perfect.

"Autumn, did our time at the resort mean more to you than I thought?" *Ugh.* He wished he could grab those thoughtless words and shove them back into his mouth. They'd both had sound reasons not to turn their amazing day into something long term.

But then he noticed tears spring into her eyes. Before she could lift her hand, one slid down her cheek. She quickly flicked it away, but he had seen it. Baby placed a paw on Autumn's chin and seemed to stare at her owner like she was worried.

Apparently, he had wounded her back then. But how?

An awkward silence descended on them while she tried to compose herself and he attempted to figure out what was happening. He racked his brain, but he could only come up with breathtaking memories. The spectacular snorkeling, followed by pool volleyball and boogie board surfing. They'd had a ton of fun and gotten to know each other during their incredible time together.

Baby shifted, so that she had a paw on each of Autumn's shoulders, as though the dog were giving her owner a hug. Cows mooed in the distance like everything was normal. But it wasn't.

Autumn snuck a glance at him and he could almost see the wheels turning in her head: *Could she trust him?* Oh, he knew all about how difficult it was to trust and how easily people could break your confidence. She swallowed and then straightened.

"You weren't there for me," she snapped.

He reared back. "What do you mean?"

"I got pregnant."

Pregnant. He felt like he'd been sucker punched in the gut. He reached for her, but she shook him off. "Oh no," he said. "I bet you tried to contact me, didn't you?" Why hadn't he sent her one last text containing his local Texas number before he ditched the disposable phone? He could have done that and still not saved her number. That would have been the courteous thing to do. But that hadn't occurred to him.

Her lips flattened as she studied him and then scowled. "I did," she bit out, while Baby made a small whining noise. "I called and sent text messages and heard nothing back." Raw pain radiated from her heated words.

"Autumn, I'm so sorry," he said. His chest squeezed that he'd put her in that predicament. "While at the resort, they gave everyone in the bridal party a disposable prepaid international phone so we could communicate but not be hit with fees. When you and I sent text messages back and forth, the number you stored for me was not my Texas number. I thought you knew that."

She appeared confused and then shook her head in disbelief.

"I'm so sorry," he repeated. His emotions swirled at her clear irritation with him. He couldn't believe she'd reached out to him and he hadn't been there for her. He scrubbed a palm over his face. "I apologize. I know we both had our reasons for not wanting a relationship, but I should have thought to give you my actual contact information." He didn't want to tell her how tempted he'd been to save her information.

She glanced at him and nodded, her features softening. A little. Which allowed him to concentrate on the monumental news she'd just laid on him. Pregnant?

The layers of shock he felt were being peeled back one at a time, but first he had to make sure she understood he hadn't purposefully ignored her.

"Had I received the messages, I would have called you back, Autumn. I promise."

She lifted her chin. He could tell she was still processing the miscommunication. Hopefully, they'd get over his innocent blunder. But, pregnant?

"Did you have the baby?" He peeked behind her as if she'd had a child all along and he hadn't even noticed. Which was crazy because he'd never seen her with a kid.

"I had a miscarriage. At five months." Hurt covered her face.

Five months seemed pretty far along. He felt so responsible. He *was* responsible. Things had gone too far their evening together.

He was trying to wrap his brain around this news. *An unexpected pregnancy and then a miscarriage?*

Autumn reached for him, but then likely thought better of it and pulled her hand back. Instead, she pressed a kiss against Baby's head. "Are you all right?" she asked. "I didn't mean to spring this on you, but I guess I assumed you knew I had tried to contact you and you chose to reject me."

"No, Autumn, I would never do that to anyone."

Anger flashed in her eyes. "I was twenty-one, and entirely alone."

Regret needled at him but then he remembered her huge comforting family. "I'm so sorry I wasn't there for you. But then with the miscarriage, I'm sure you told—"

"My family?" she interrupted him. "No way. I was full of shame." Her eyes filled with tears, and Baby whined again. "I couldn't tell anyone, especially them. I guess that's why I was so mad at you. You were really the only person I could have talked to."

He stumbled back. Suddenly this landing felt way too small. His regret turned into frustration that he'd not had the foresight to give her his real contact info.

No wonder she hadn't wanted to work with him when he first arrived at the Triple C. It explained the reason she'd acted funny around him, like she was upset with him. Because she was.

His gaze flew to her pretty, albeit teary, face. He couldn't believe she'd reached out to him and he hadn't been there for her.

She'd gone through the pregnancy and then a second trimester miscarriage all by herself because he'd made a stupid mistake.

Could he ever forgive himself for being so careless?
Perhaps more importantly, could she ever forgive him?

"Autumn?" Wyatt touched her hand. She flinched. He
removed his fingers as Baby turned and glared at him as
though she wanted to growl or maybe snap at him for hurting her owner. Autumn kissed her terrier for her faithful-
ness, especially during this trying time.

"Are you okay?" he asked. "You look like you're going
to pass out. You should sit."

She gave him a hard shake of her head and focused on
the cattle grazing in the pasture beyond him. This conversation was about to do her in. She tried to ignore the appeal of his scent, a hint of wood, earth and hard work, as
it floated between them. She clutched Baby a little closer.
What would she have done the past six years without her
terrier? Especially today.

All Autumn wanted to do was turn and flee, but she'd
been waiting for this moment for years. If she didn't speak
up, she'd never forgive herself. She lifted her chin and gazed
into his handsome face. "You hurt me, Wyatt. You left me
pregnant and alone, and didn't bother to answer my calls."
When Wyatt attempted to defend himself, she placed her
hand up like a stop sign. The words of pain were bubbling
up, fighting for a chance to be heard.

"I hear you," she said. "You had a disposable phone. I
didn't have your real number. But the point of the matter
is, you abandoned me to deal with a pregnancy and then
a supremely difficult miscarriage. I was twenty-one, and
you left me in a situation without support from anyone."
She sucked in a shaky breath. "Not only was I pregnant
and left alone to deal with the fallout, you actually went on
with your life. Got promotions and raises. Had a success-

ful career. Met a woman and married her. Had an adorable child." Her voice cracked with emotion at how he'd lived. Yet, she'd never been able to turn the page on that chapter of her past. The past that seemed to define her. It all felt so unfair.

She looked him in the eye to tell him the raw truth. "Maybe I shouldn't be, Wyatt, but I'm angry with you. The whole situation is just not fair. Not at all." Boy, that felt good. She was angry and he deserved to know.

"That's completely understandable. I'd be angry as well. Probably furious."

His agreeing with her kind of took the wind out of her sails. She sighed and considered what he had said about the phone he'd been using. Now that he'd reminded her about the texting fees, she recalled the enormous phone bill she had received after that getaway. She also had a vague memory of overhearing someone else in the bridal party commenting about the disposable phones they'd been gifted.

That explained why there was no personalized voicemail greeting on his number and why he hadn't responded.

"I'm sorry, Autumn," he said. "You honestly tried to reach me and I can see where you thought I was ignoring you, but I wasn't." Regret now covered Wyatt's features as he leaned against the deck railing, still stunned at her news. Clad in a sawdust-covered tee and worn blue jeans, he was solid muscle and looked better than a man ought to.

Since she had been living with a friend in Dallas, she hadn't returned home during the pregnancy. She hadn't thought things could get worse, then she'd had the miscarriage. As the memories rushed back, she dug her fingers into Baby's comforting fur.

After she was released from the hospital, she had landed a job at a doggie day care. She planned to stay away from family and try to heal from the experience. But about a year later, still broken, she'd met Baby at a local animal shelter where she volunteered on the weekends to keep herself busy. The day she wrote up the intake papers on the Jack Russell, she had adopted her. But when she returned to the apartment with a dog, her roommate reminded her about the no pet policy, which forced Autumn to return to the Triple C before she had planned.

She put Baby down on the landing. Technically, neither of them was in the wrong, but she was still upset at how he'd snubbed her back then, even if he hadn't meant it. She believed she had his number and made her best attempt at contacting him. He hadn't thought about the ramifications of using a disposable phone. It was all in the past, she'd best move on.

But could she?

She lowered her right foot to the first tread, hoping Wyatt didn't see her movement as the escape tactic it was. Baby hopped down the step and leaned against her ankle in a show of support.

Now that he knew the truth, and she'd discovered she hadn't had his correct contact information, she should leave. There was nothing left to discuss. He didn't need to know how upset she was that he hadn't been there for her. All the nights she had cried herself to sleep. The emotional turmoil after she had returned home from the hospital to recover.

Not to mention the distance this enormous secret had created between her and her loved ones. Maybe she should have been brave enough to tell them, but she had been young and afraid. The more time that passed, the harder it had been to come clean. So she'd simply kept it buried and lived with the wall she had erected between herself and her family.

"Really, Autumn, I wasn't trying to avoid you." The way he gazed at her made her uncomfortable because she wasn't sure she was ready to forgive and forget. At least not yet. Baby stood on her hind legs and put her paws on Autumn's thigh. She patted her companion's head.

When Autumn didn't respond, he continued. "Thank you for sharing what happened." His quiet voice rumbled between them, sparking an interest she desired to remain buried. "It couldn't have been easy to rehash that difficult time. The other day when we reconnected, I could tell you had changed. I immediately saw a new confidence, but I wasn't sure the cause. Now I know." The pain etched on his tanned features just about broke her, and she so wanted to pick up Baby and snuggle close. Instead she focused on the field in the distance dotted with grazing cows. She and Wyatt were both in agony, but for different reasons.

She peeked at him and saw him intently studying her. He held her gaze, and she was unable to look away.

Right then, something strange sparked between them and it scared her. She fisted her hands at her sides, feeling much too vulnerable in his sight. She wanted to flee now more than ever.

He ran his palm over his attractive high and tight hair. "I was a little wild during that time in my life and I'm sorry things got to where they did."

She offered him a tight nod. If only they hadn't, so much would be different today. For starters, she wouldn't feel like such a failure.

She realized that telling him the truth had healed a corner of her heart and relief swooshed through her. But before she could revel in the healing, she recognized their conversation had inexplicably drawn her closer to him. Which wasn't her intention at all.

He might not have been there seven years ago, but he was here now. Something about spilling her guts had actually helped.

She was grateful he realized how much it had cost her. Whether or not he knew it, his compassion went a long way to helping her forgive him and soothe her jumbled feelings.

"I hope you don't mind my asking, but is Baby your emotional support dog? She seems very in tune with you."

Autumn swallowed a lump in her throat at the mere thought of not having Baby by her side. "Yes. I mean, she wasn't originally trained, she's just really compassionate. I adopted her about a year after my hospital stay, and I think God gave her to me for comfort during that time."

"So when you took her to training so she could visit children's hospitals, she was already working for you as an ESA?"

"Yes. She was the inspiration for my business." Autumn reached down and scratched the top of Baby's head. "When we were at the resort, you were against a relationship. If you don't mind my asking, what changed?"

"After my grandmother's health scare, I worked some things out. I had finally gotten to a place where a relationship didn't petrify me. Then a few years after we were on the island, I met Chloe." His expression became tension-filled. "After my wife's accident and Harper's emergency delivery, I came to believe in God. Autumn, I really need to ask for your forgiveness. My actions, our actions, put you in a difficult position. Will you forgive me?"

"Yes, I forgive you." She found the heartfelt acceptance was easier than she thought it'd be, so she focused on the faith part of what he'd said. "The pregnancy forced me to evaluate my life, and I also became a believer." Though after the miscarriage, she pushed God away for a while, confident He had been judging her actions. Some days she still believed that.

"I was wondering," he said. "I can see a tremendous difference in you since we were together at the resort."

She hated to admit it, but he seemed different as well. He seemed more willing to listen. His sparkling eyes held more patience. Of course, seeing him as a dad just about undid her. She'd never seen another father as tender with his words. Somehow that attracted her.

Her eyes widened. She had embraced her call to singleness, so what was happening here?

Right before she'd gone on that island vacation, her long-time boyfriend had dumped her and then Wyatt hadn't answered the most important call of his life. Those things together had made Autumn believe she wasn't capable of having a successful relationship. She wasn't important enough for others to stick around.

She knew that once any man got to know her and realized how unimpressive she was, they'd discard her.

She lowered both feet to the top step. The realization that he hadn't ignored her and hadn't rejected her began to soothe a broken part of her heart. But she itched to get away from him and the confession, and ponder all these new revelations.

"Wyatt, I'd appreciate it if you never brought this up again," she stated, then turned and rushed down the stairs, Baby at her heels.

Once in the safety of her barn, the barking dogs calmed her as she swiped at her damp cheeks. Her phone dinged with a text.

Henry Wright.

I just wanted to let you know I'm retiring and moving to Florida, so I'm listing my ranch. If I sell, I'm unsure if the new owner will let you use the barn. Will keep you posted.

No! No, no, no. Without this barn, her business would fail. Her mind twirled with the other dog barn options she'd previously considered and abandoned. All the Triple C barns were in use, so there was no space to run a business in any of them. Her parents' garage was a possibility, but the constant barking, especially at night, would bother her parents, and she didn't want to do that to them. Henry's place was it.

Her gaze flitted to Wyatt, who'd returned to replacing the rotted boards. Now she'd have to focus on earning money to prove to the new owner that leasing to her was worth it.

She sank onto a hay bale. Baby jumped into her lap and put her paws on Autumn's shoulders.

Autumn pressed her forehead against Baby's. "I didn't think things could get worse, sweetheart, but they have."

Chapter Five

Her mother started the mixer, but the hum of the appliance did nothing to soothe Autumn's nerves. She *had* to tell her about the pregnancy and miscarriage or this guilt she carried would eat her alive. This secret had built a wall between her and her loved ones, her mother especially. But her mother would be so disappointed Autumn had found herself in that predicament to begin with. Except now that Wyatt knew, she had to tell her family. Family trumped an ex-boyfriend, or whatever he was.

The enticing smell of baked goods and notes of sweet lemon filled the kitchen as Autumn screwed up the courage to speak.

The mixer turned off and her mother leveled Autumn with a warm stare she didn't feel she deserved. "I can tell something is on your mind, sweetheart. Did you need to talk?"

Trepidation and nervousness warred within at what she was about to tell her mother. Seemed like the secret had grown larger each year and built the wall between them higher and higher. When she was released from the hospital, she should have told her mother. But she had panicked and taken the easy way out by remaining silent.

"Henry's selling," Autumn blurted out the first thing that popped into her head. She couldn't tell her mother her secret, could she? Yes, she could, but she just didn't have the guts. Not now at least. It seemed Autumn had a problem being open and vulnerable with the people she cared about.

"Really?" her mother responded. "Ever since his wife passed, I'd heard rumors he might move to Florida." She used a spatula to scrape all the batter off the twisted wire whip attachment. "Did he say anything about your leased barn?"

"Just that it would be up in the air." *Tell her about your past. She loves you and, even though you felt shame about what happened, she deserves to know. And you deserve to recapture the close bond you once had with her.*

Her mother sympathized and gave her a few suggestions, but Autumn had already considered and dismissed them.

The boldness she'd walked into the kitchen with dwindled the longer the Henry-is-selling conversation continued.

"How's the Serenity Days Arts and Crafts Festival going?" her mother asked. "If you need help, you know we're here for you."

Autumn teared up at the support her mother and entire family constantly gave her. Fortunately they didn't appear to notice the distance between them, or at least they chose not to address it.

"I sent my booth application in on the very last day, so hopefully we'll get a space outside the tent, or one on the end so we'll have access to the grass and be outside for the demonstrations." She couldn't believe she'd almost missed the deadline. Hopefully they would get a booth that would work for the dogs and Wyatt's demonstrations.

She turned the Bundt pan as her mother poured in the thick mixture. After her mother placed the cake in the oven and set a timer, Autumn took her leave. How come she always ended up caving to the fear that held her hostage?

Her head throbbed with the burdensome secret sitting on her tongue waiting to be unleashed.

Telling her mother would be hard, but it was the first step in rebuilding their fractured relationship. She shook her head. But not today.

When the screen door slapped behind her, she stepped onto her parent's porch and pushed all thoughts of the pregnancy and miscarriage away. It was in the past. Where it belonged.

Baby sat waiting and barked when she spotted her owner.

When Autumn heard her terrier, the tension coiled in her chest unraveled. She knelt down and gathered Baby into her arms, clutching her furry companion close.

As she walked down the front steps, Henry passed the ranch and honked. She gave him a little wave as he continued on his way.

What was she going to do if he sold and the new owner wouldn't let her lease her barn? She groaned. Not only was she going to have to rely on Wyatt, he'd probably leave this position once he paid off his debt and no longer needed the apartment exchange. Then she wouldn't have a dog trainer anymore and likely wouldn't be able to pay a salary.

Treading toward the dog barn, she paused and released Baby to join her friends. Why was Barbara, one of her therapy dog clients, here? She passed the sparkling white minivan and quickened her steps. Maybe Barbara had questions. Or she was pulling out of her commitment to purchase Tallulah once she was trained. Autumn hadn't thought of having her clients sign a contract. Indecision hummed in her brain.

As she neared the dog barn, she heard voices, including Wyatt's. Her pulse sped up at his chuckle. For three days, each time an opportunity arose to talk, she'd made herself scarce, afraid he'd corner her and want to talk about the past. Now the tension between them was thick enough to cut with a knife.

She entered the barn. Barbara and her five-year-old son, Tanner, stood with Wyatt in a circle, chatting like old friends.

Autumn engulfed the older woman in a hug and offered her palm to Tanner for a high five.

"Barbara, I see you've met Wyatt, the dog trainer I was telling you about."

"Yes, I did. I was welcoming him to Serenity," her client said. "I'm thrilled you're now on the team, Wyatt, and excited to see what Tallulah has learned."

Okay. Barbara had every right to see the progress of her diabetic service dog, but why hadn't she contacted Autumn? She felt bad she hadn't even been around to greet her client when she had arrived.

"Sure. Absolutely," Autumn said. She reached for Tallulah's crate door right as Wyatt did. She pulled her hand away as though she had just touched a burning cooktop.

A pleasant fluttery sensation bubbled in her stomach. *Stop. This is Wyatt. He means nothing to you.*

The memory of her confession to him three days ago popped into her head but she firmly pushed it away. She had to get it together because she had a business to run.

"Go ahead," she said as she waved toward Tallulah.

"Thanks." He opened the door, hooked a leash on the dog and took her out the exit leading to the outdoor pens. Autumn scurried after him while Barbara crouched down to speak with Tanner.

While Barbara and Tanner were inside having a discussion, Autumn joined Wyatt.

"I'm kind of excited," he said.

Butterflies raced around her stomach. She worked to tamp them down. "Same here."

None of the awkwardness that had plagued them the past few days persisted. Maybe she'd just assumed he'd want to talk more about the past. Either way, she was glad, at least in this moment, that things felt normal between them again. Well, except her fluttery stomach.

"Tanner looks well-adjusted," Wyatt whispered.

"He is when he has family around, but being on his own at school makes him nervous," she responded. "Tallulah is going to give him the confidence he needs when he doesn't have his support system around him."

Through the tall pines, Autumn spotted Harper with the twins in Laney's backyard. She appreciated Wyatt didn't want any interruptions during their time with Barbara and Tanner, but how had he set up that playdate so quickly?

Barbara's wide smile and the skip in Tanner's step proved they were excited as well.

"I thought we'd put Tallulah through some commands so you can see her progression," Wyatt said. Good thing he was so professional, what with Barbara just dropping in unannounced.

Her client's eyes danced at his statement. They'd been talking about this moment for months, and now it was here. Who cared if it wasn't a scheduled visit?

As Wyatt put Tallulah through the hoops, Barbara gave little claps of excitement and Autumn grinned.

Next Wyatt placed the empty cinder block, which he'd duct-taped so the dog wouldn't get her snout scratched, on the platform and waited until Tallulah jumped onto the elevated surface and then stuck her nose in the block and sniffed. He released the dog and immediately treated her.

Barbara's face shone with delight at the first step in scent detection.

This was why Autumn had started her business. Once he had Tallulah by his side, little Tanner would be able to lead a confident life.

It amazed Autumn how much Wyatt had taught Tallulah in just a week. Even though her rapport with Wyatt had been tense, she'd secured the best possible trainer for the job.

Barbara lifted on her toes. "Tallulah has progressed by leaps and bounds since the last time I saw her. I'm so excited Wyatt is here to start the scent detection."

Autumn exhaled the nervous breath she hadn't realized she'd been holding and looked up at Wyatt. If their partnership worked, her business would succeed.

Wyatt glanced at her and grinned, and her heart flip-flopped. Yes, things were still a little awkward between the two of them, but somehow her honesty had healed her, if just a little. Maybe the two of them could move on from the past and develop a good working relationship.

When he was done with the demonstration, Wyatt crouched low to let Tanner pet Tallulah. "I can tell these two know each other and already get along well. That'll help with the transition."

"They do, and I appreciate you calling to invite us today," Barbara said.

Autumn straightened. Wyatt had gone behind her back and contacted one of her clients without consulting her first? Confusion and anger whirred within.

Wyatt stood. "You are welcome, but the real reason I called you here today was to explain that Tallulah can't be ready by the July first date Autumn promised."

Autumn snapped her head in his direction, but schooled

her face. Wyatt had contacted her client. Without consulting her. Fury built up. "But—"

"As the certified dog trainer, I know the steps Tallulah needs to go through between now and then, and there just aren't enough hours in the day to meet that deadline." He explained that not only did Tallulah need specialized training to be a scent-trained dog, but Wyatt would need to work with Barbara and Tanner as well to set them up for success.

Autumn was furious with him for speaking with a client before talking with her first. Though, as he talked about the promised date, she realized she had overlooked Tanner's young age. Yes, she had included time to train the client, but hadn't added extra time to account for his youth. She definitely wanted the handoff done right, and if she hadn't brought Wyatt in, maybe she'd be jeopardizing her entire business.

Though she respected Wyatt's knowledge and how he was sticking up for what would ultimately work best for Tanner, she was irritated with how Wyatt went about telling her client this news.

She had jumped at hiring Wyatt because he was her only option, but if he was going to lean hard into perfectionism, maybe she had selected the wrong trainer. Her business goal was to succeed, but right now it seemed he might be her road to failure.

Was he purposefully sabotaging her business?

Autumn hugged Barbara and high-fived Tanner, then the duo trudged to their minivan. Though she was smiling at her client, the tension since Wyatt stated they would not meet Autumn's delivery date for Tallulah was massive. If steam could actually rise from someone's head, Autumn's would be sizzling.

Wyatt scrubbed a hand over his freshly shaven chin. Maybe he'd overstepped?

No. Autumn had promised Barbara a fully trained date for Tallulah before she'd even met him. If that wasn't hasty decision-making skills, he didn't know what was. Because of that, he wasn't sure he could trust Autumn. He was unsure about tying his good name to hers if her plan was to operate a fly-by-night operation and not take this business seriously.

His mother would call him distrustful and always looking for ulterior motives, but in this case, he felt justified.

Except Autumn's angry stance made him pause. Maybe he could have handled this situation a little better. They were kind of partners after all.

Earlier, when they'd both reached for Tallulah's crate at the same time and their fingers had touched, something electric had passed between them. He shook off the memory. She was his boss and held the keys to the apartment his daughter loved so much.

Barbara backed out of the parking space and waved as she drove away.

"Don't ever contact one of my clients behind my back again," Autumn said through gritted teeth. Then she whirled, her tumble of hair fanning her face which was a combination of hurt and anger. "Understand?"

"Hey, calm down. My reputation's on the line here and—"

"Daddy." Harper dashed into the barn, her face full of excitement. "I had the bestest morning ever."

From the grassy field, Laney, wearing a front carrier with her two-month-old in it, wiggled her fingers at them, joined hands with her twins and headed into her home. Boy, she had a lot on her plate. He'd have to thank her yet again for watching Harper, through a text message instead of bothering her right now.

"We petted the goats and the chickens and did you know they have miniature ponies? I want one. We could keep it in the bathtub."

Wyatt chuckled. "We are not getting a miniature pony. But I'm glad you had a good time."

"Where's Buster?"

"He's in the first pen with the big dogs," Autumn said. "You can go in with them if you want to see him."

"Thanks," Harper stated as she rushed through the barn, opened the ten-by-ten pen door, slipped through with no dogs escaping and then clicked it closed behind her.

For some reason, his daughter had fallen in love with Buster, one of the service dogs in training. He wasn't sure what Harper would do when the border collie left the ranch.

He could feel Autumn's angry gaze on him, but he had worked too hard on his dog training career to give it all up for some pretty woman.

"Okay," he relented. "I apologize for contacting Barbara without speaking to you first. But I've been trying to tell you we won't hit Tallulah's date, and you don't seem to hear me." At his apology, her tense body seemed to relax a notch and she unclenched her hands. Her expression even softened a bit. Well, at least the awkwardness that had almost been a third person between them ever since she had told him about the pregnancy and miscarriage was gone. Replaced for now with her irritation at him contacting Barbara.

Harper rushed into the barn, the border collie and Baby close behind. "Buster didn't want to be closed in."

Autumn's features softened at Harper's cute comment while Wyatt chuckled.

Baby slowed to check on her owner. Autumn crouched

low and gave the dog an aggressive back rub, which the terrier leaned into. Then Baby stuck her snout in Autumn's face and they gently rubbed noses. That seemed to be the dog's way of making sure Autumn was okay and she could go play.

His daughter hugged his leg and then rushed after the collie. At least he had Harper and her cute antics, otherwise Autumn might fire him.

Harper plopped onto the grass and picked a daisy, the McCaws even had nice flowering weeds in their grass, and started plucking the white petals off one by one. Her lips were moving, so he knew she was playing the *he loves me, he loves me not* game. She had learned it in day care from a girl with an older sister.

"She's adorable, and so sweet. You've done a wonderful job raising her." Autumn's voice had gone all mushy, like it usually did when she talked about his delightful daughter. They'd been fast friends ever since she'd offered to pick up Harper from day care that one afternoon.

He was grateful his daughter was living a carefree life at this ranch and was indebted to Autumn for the apartment and country life they'd been given. "Thank you. Moving here has helped her disposition immensely, so thank you for extending the job offer to me. She's almost made it a whole day at day care, and I think this serene ranch has something to do with it."

"I'm glad for her," she said. "Tallulah is doing great. What's the next step for advancing her scent-detecting skills?" Her tone was all business. Clearly, she was doing what she could to put him contacting her client behind her, which he appreciated.

"Next she'll encounter a larger number of empty containers, Winston too."

"Nice. How does that work?"

"I set up the receptacles and I'll want them to place their nose in each empty container, to show interest in the task."

She looked pleased. But then something crossed over her face, and his stomach plummeted. "What's wrong?"

"The deadline probably doesn't matter," Autumn said, "since my business won't make it."

He whipped his head around, her statement slicing a knife into his chest. "What?"

She told him that her landlord was selling his property, and she didn't know if the new owner would allow her to lease the barn.

"This structure is so far away from his other barns and his house, I can't imagine the new owner ousting you," he replied. "But if we get that news, we'll find somewhere else." He caught her uncertain gaze. "I'm military and we never give up."

Her eyes filled with moisture that she promptly swiped away. He was thrilled to have made her happy, for once. Baby sidled up to her, she picked up her dog and buried her nose in her fur. "Thanks, Wyatt."

She was gorgeous, courageous, persistent, a hard worker and loved kids. Maybe, when they previously met, it hadn't been the right time. Anyway, after his hair-raising divorce, he wasn't interested in another relationship. With anyone.

Right then, two gold streaks whizzed past them. Panic filled him at spotting the loose boarding dogs.

Autumn sucked in a breath and then raced after them. "I've got them," she called as she ran toward the docile brothers, calling their names.

He stood frozen in place as she gathered the two big dogs from the first pen where Harper had just snagged Buster from. His daughter must not have securely closed the latch.

He'd talk with her later. Right now, he scrambled over to check on the other dogs.

Sure enough, the gate was wide-open, though Winston, the golden retriever diabetic alert dog, was sitting in the center of the pen at attention. "Good boy," he said as he quickly closed and locked the gate. Where was Luna? The Australian Shepherd wasn't in her designated crate in the dog barn, so she must have been in one of the outdoor pens. A quick scan of the other two spaces proved she wasn't there.

Barking in the distance caught his attention. Across the way he saw Luna trying to herd a couple of cows.

He raced across the pasture, hoping the bull in the corner didn't decide to charge after him, and chased after the Aussie but to no avail. She was in her element. Panting, he crouched low and held his hand out like he had a treat. Falling for his trick, Luna ran over and he grabbed the hook on the dog's harness to pick her up. He grunted at her heft. She wasn't light, but there was no way he was trusting her to follow him.

As he neared the enclosures, Autumn was closing the brothers in.

"Thank you," she said, relief covering her features at the dog in his arms. "Where was Luna?"

He slipped the runner into the pen. "Chasing the cows."

Her gaze shifted to the pasture and then back to him. "That bull in there is aggressive. I'm surprised he didn't chase after you."

His eyebrows lifted in surprise. Maybe it was a good thing he hadn't known that. "The dogs are safe now. That's all that matters," he said and followed her back through the barn, where she checked out all the crates as though cataloging all the pups in her head. A nod seemed to say she was satisfied with her count.

"Sorry about that fiasco," he said. "I'll talk with Harper later about making sure she latches the gate behind herself."

"No problem, an innocent mistake," she said and returned to their spot in the shade where he could monitor his daughter, Buster nearby. Somehow, Baby had ended up in Autumn's arms. "I should stop boarding my friends' dogs as favors."

He was thankful she was so understanding about the dogs getting loose under Harper's watch. "You need to treat your business like a business or you'll never get ahead." But he kind of liked her soft heart. It made Autumn into the woman he was growing very fond of.

His gaze drifted to the little landing outside his apartment door, but he didn't need that space to remind him of the talk they had a few days ago. He was thankful Autumn had been truthful with him, albeit a little late. He felt bad she'd gone through that experience and hoped they could get to a less awkward working relationship.

But mostly he felt bad that their actions seemed to have changed the outcome of Autumn's life. He wasn't sure why, but something about that situation still haunted Autumn, which made him unsure how to act around her. But avoiding her wasn't working, it was just making things more uncomfortable.

"I feel so bad about the baby. The miscarriage."

She flashed a look at Harper playing with Buster nearby. "Keep your voice down."

"She can't hear us," he spoke a notch above a whisper.

Autumn blew a strand of honey-blond hair from her face and pinned him with a look. Her soulful emerald eyes seemed to plead with him. "I don't want to talk about it, Wyatt." Her lip trembled, but her voice grew stronger with each word she spoke. "We just spent some time together. We weren't really dating or anything."

He glimpsed Harper directly behind Autumn. His daughter's eyes rounded in surprise at Autumn's comment about dating, while his heart leaped into his throat. How long had she been there? Had she heard anything? He gulped at the notion of Harper spreading any of what she may have overheard.

But as quick as she'd appeared, she took off chasing after the border collie and he turned his attention back to Autumn.

"I'm just so sorry about not returning your calls and texts," he said. That experience had molded her. Made her a stronger, more focused individual. One he respected more and more with each passing day. And those new emotions scared him.

"Trust me, I'm over it." She clutched Baby a little harder, turned and fled to the dog runs.

But Autumn running didn't surprise Wyatt. That seemed to be her defense mechanism.

What did surprise him was how much he was beginning to care for her.

Their discussion from a few days ago had created an unbreakable bond between them. Did she feel it too?

Except he'd been burned by trusting others in the past.

He believed the closer someone got to him, the higher likelihood they could hurt him.

His only option was to keep his relationship with Autumn all business. That way, no one would get hurt.

Chapter Six

$\sim\!\!\diamondsuit\!\!\sim$

Wyatt was almost giddy when he pulled open the day care door on Monday afternoon. The director hadn't contacted him to talk with a worried-but-not-yet-unglued Harper. Not one meltdown. Not one call for Harper to be picked up. The first day that he hadn't received a distressed call or had to pick her up in more than two weeks.

He nodded at another father who'd just arrived. Wyatt had an impulse to chest bump the man to celebrate his daughter's day, but refrained himself.

In the corner, Harper scanned a toy food box at the supermarket play set. Another girl stood close by with a loaded shopping cart. They were both grinning.

The director approached him. "Harper had a great day," she said.

Instantly, he decided that Harper's accomplishment deserved a celebration, but what? He didn't want to make a big deal out of it to Harper, but he was proud of his daughter. She didn't like change. She'd lived through trauma with her mother this past year and come out the other side stronger and happier.

The minute Harper spotted him, she dropped her toys and ran to him. He grabbed her and spun her around, enjoying the feeling of completing a hard day's work, knowing his child had been happy and well cared for while they were apart.

As he carried her out to the truck and placed her in her car seat, she chattered about her day. The sound of her happy babbling touched him. She sounded truly content, and he had Serenity and the Triple C Ranch apartment to thank for her happiness.

"Did you know today marks my third week at Mighty Paws?" He leaned over and fastened the seat belt around Harper like he used to when she was younger. "How about we go to Mabel's Diner to celebrate?"

She clapped. "Yay! I can get a grilled cheese with the yellow kind I like so much."

He lifted his palm for a high five and then settled in the driver's seat to buckle in. Her happiness permeated the truck and Wyatt reveled in the moment.

"Can we invite Miss Autumn to meet us? It won't feel like a celebration without her."

His stomach jolted at the mention of Autumn's name. They'd fallen into an agreeable dog training routine in the evenings. Sure, they chatted about topics other than dogs. But if he invited her to dinner tonight, they wouldn't have the dogs as a buffer, and that troubled him.

"I'm sure she has plans. This is very last-minute."

"Can't we at least try?" A glance in the rearview mirror showed Harper's bottom lip sticking out with a plea.

How could he say no to her? She'd gone through so much, and tonight was a victory dinner.

"Please?" She strung the word out as though it had ten syllables.

Despite Autumn giving him the dog trainer job and picking up Harper on a number of occasions so he could keep working, he wasn't keen about depending on her, or anyone. Especially because she wouldn't always be around, so he didn't want his daughter to invest herself too much in Autumn. His little girl had been through so much with the antics of her mother.

Another glance in the rearview mirror cracked his resolve. "Okay," he said, then shot Autumn a text and drove into downtown, securing an angled spot along the town square. Though he had enjoyed his time in San Antonio, this small town had won him over. Their close-knit community, the slower pace and the adorable downtown area that felt safe and homey. It was perfect for raising a young child.

He glanced at his phone. Maybe Autumn would decline since it was such short notice.

His phone dinged with a positive response. He frowned, then texted back to meet them at the toy store.

He hoped sharing this celebratory dinner with her wouldn't become too personal because he really wanted to keep things between them strictly professional.

"Autumn can come. She'll meet us at the toy store where we are browsing," he said as he eyed his daughter unlatching her seat belt. "We won't be purchasing anything today, young lady." She nodded at him.

They strolled through the town, then entered the toy store. His daughter raced from display to display, playing with all the available toys. She finally landed at the doll aisle, where she played with a doll that wailed if she wasn't sucking on a bottle. He focused on his phone to catch up with emails he'd missed during the day.

Fifteen minutes later, he placed the doll on the counter next to the cash register. Yes, he'd told Harper no purchases today, but after her successful day, she deserved a treat.

He handed the clerk a twenty as the door chimed with a new customer. When he looked up, his gaze locked on Autumn, and her eyes sparkled with excitement as she stepped over the toy store threshold. He suddenly realized that inviting her hadn't been a mistake. She was part of the reason he still had his job with Doc Earl, because she'd been so helpful in picking up Harper from day care when needed.

The wide smile on her heart-shaped face did something to his insides. Her hair, usually in a ponytail, cascaded in waves around her shoulders, like it had been curled and styled special for tonight. She was always pretty, but this evening she was breathtaking.

She lifted a hand to wave, and Harper barreled into her. Autumn threw her head back to laugh and then picked up Harper, placing her on her hip as if they'd known each other for years.

"Where's Baby?" Harper asked, looking behind Autumn as though the dog was playing hide-and-seek.

"She can't come into stores and restaurants, silly. But when we get back to the Triple C, you can give her a special treat. How about that?" Autumn asked, ever so thoughtful.

His heart squeezed at how much his daughter admired the woman. He admired her as well. Driven, focused and fun to be with. Lately, they'd been spending so much time together that they'd been sharing snippets of their past as they worked together. The more he learned, the more he liked.

He joined them. "Ready for dinner?"

After they left the toy store, he took Harper's hand while holding the doll bag in his other.

His daughter snagged Autumn's hand, so the three of them made a chain on the sidewalk. The way his daughter had taken to Autumn warmed his heart, yet scared him at the same time. Harper connected too quickly to people, so when they departed from her life, it wounded her. She'd had enough pain in her short lifetime.

"I want a mommy like you, Miss Autumn," Harper stated in a cheery voice.

Wyatt stumbled on a sidewalk crack, but he righted himself before falling. A lump formed in his throat at the turbulent relationship Harper had with her now-incarcerated mother. This was the first time Harper had mentioned wanting another mother, and her simple words shredded Wyatt.

Autumn looked down at Harper with her lips in a grim line. "You are such a sweetie," she said, but she didn't look happy with the pronouncement.

The trio shuffled around a group of people standing and chatting on the sidewalk. He glimpsed Autumn as she nibbled on her lower lip, appearing agitated, and he felt horrible. She had shared how returning from the hospital empty-handed, with no chance of being a mother to their baby, had traumatized her. To this day, she struggled with women announcing pregnancies or being around infants. Harper's comment must have opened that wound and he felt responsible.

Once at the diner, he held the door open and Harper skipped in. When Autumn passed by, their gazes met and he saw a flash of deep pain cover her face. Her expression hollowed him out and made him lose his appetite.

He touched her lower back to guide her to Harper's favorite booth, but also to let her know she wasn't alone anymore. Her floral perfume wafted in the air between them. They were a team. Not only in dog training but in dealing with the past. He'd help her anyway he could since he hadn't been there when she needed him.

He slid into the booth as Harper knelt on the vinyl bench seat and discussed her meal options with Autumn, who sat against the wall and gave his daughter all her attention. Autumn's features, void of the hurt and dismay from a few moments ago, were full of excitement over chatting with his daughter.

Her passionate interest in everything Harper had to say turned his insides to jelly.

He stilled. Why was he thinking of Autumn romantically? Hadn't he decided to keep it strictly professional?

Autumn settled on the bench seat beside Harper, still reeling from the little girl's earlier words, *I want a mommy like you*.

At twenty-one, when she had lost her baby, she'd decided she wouldn't make a good mother and didn't deserve a second chance. Had she stayed away from relationships because she was afraid of getting married, discovering herself pregnant and then losing another baby the same way? If she were honest with herself, she was fearful her body couldn't handle carrying a baby to full term.

Lord, please take away my fear.

"I'm getting the grilled cheese," Harper lowered her voice for the next part. "They use the yummy yellow cheese that Daddy won't buy."

Autumn grinned and suppressed a chuckle. This girl had the biggest personality. She'd almost said no to the invite, but because she imagined the request was coming from Harper, she couldn't turn it down. She'd grown fond of the girl over these past weeks.

She lifted her wavy hair off her neck. She never should have let Trisha, her newest sister-in-law, and her two girls give her a makeover. Thankfully, she'd washed the makeup off her face before she hopped in her car. But other than washing her hair, she was stuck with these fancy waves that absolutely didn't fit her personality.

The dinner invite had touched her, though she knew it

wasn't Wyatt who had wanted her here. She'd read between the lines of the celebratory dinner text and figured it was because Harper had made it through the whole day at day care. When Autumn had stopped by the vet clinic midday, Wyatt had been optimistic. Not that she'd asked him. She had overheard him sharing the news with the receptionist.

She shrugged off the perplexing romantic feelings that had plagued her on the drive over. She needn't worry about sending Wyatt the wrong signals because it was clear he only wanted friendship, if even that. Which was exactly what Autumn wanted. No, the person she needed to convince that she and Wyatt would never be a couple was Harper. The little girl with dreams of a new mommy and a completed family.

If Harper only knew how scarred Autumn was, she'd run far away. But Autumn would keep her past to herself because she'd been enjoying getting to know the little girl. It couldn't hurt to add a four-year-old as a good friend, could it?

"Can I get a hot fudge sundae for dessert? Please," Harper asked, while Autumn tried not to giggle at the child's desperate request for sweets.

"Well, seeing as this is a celebratory dinner, I don't see why not." Wyatt's eyes twinkled at Harper.

The girl had shown amazing emotional growth since she'd arrived at the Triple C. Though she'd been adorable since day one, she'd been skittish. She had turned out to be an easygoing child, one Autumn enjoyed being with.

She took in Wyatt as he played tic-tac-toe with Harper across the table. His eyes were striking. The satisfied smile on his face seemed to drown out the defeated look she'd become used to seeing on him since he'd shown up at her dog barn a couple of weeks ago. Maybe Harper's issues, along with whatever had happened with his ex-wife, had been bringing him down. Perhaps the move to Serenity had been exactly what he needed to bring his life back on track.

Regardless, she was grateful for his reaction earlier, when Harper had made that statement. It was almost like he understood how painful her past was and how those words had scraped at the still-open wound.

They ordered. Autumn used a crayon to play tic-tac-toe on her paper place mat with Harper, and the girl whooped each time she won. In between games, Wyatt asked Autumn about her day, and she reciprocated. He was always easy to talk with, and they never ran out of topics to explore. Now that he knew about her past, she was glad she'd hired him because he was doing an amazing job training the dogs and she was learning a lot from his techniques.

The food arrived at the table, and he prayed for their meal. Though they'd gotten along fine this past week, there had been a barrier between them. This afternoon, when Trisha had asked about the dog training and the first thing out of Autumn's mouth was the meeting Wyatt had set up with Barbara behind her back, she knew she needed to move on from that betrayal. His intentions had been in the right place. And frankly, he'd been right. She hadn't wanted to hear him when he persisted in informing her they would not meet their first dog-in-home date. Tonight they seemed to be starting fresh, with the past where it belonged, and she was ever so thankful for that.

"Can I have a fry?" Harper asked. The grilled cheese in front of her was coupled with crinkled potato chips.

"Sure, have as many as you want."

Wyatt gave her an encouraging look, and Autumn's heart stuttered.

Her head snapped back. Uh-uh. She was not thinking of

Wyatt romantically, was she? They had too much complication in their past. She glanced at him. Or had they moved on with a clean slate?

Harper waved her sandwich back and forth.

"Too hot?" Autumn asked. "Want me to break it into pieces?"

She nodded and put the grilled cheese back on the plate.

Autumn broke the sandwich up and, for the first time in seven years, didn't lament that she'd never do this with her own child.

Somehow, meeting Harper had been freeing to Autumn's psyche. Yes, the pregnancy and miscarriage had been a difficult time in her life, but the aftereffects seemed to be dimming. All thanks to Wyatt's little girl.

When she looked up, Wyatt was studying her intently. Then he smiled at her and thanked her for helping Harper with her dinner.

"Any news with Henry Wright and your lease?" He took a massive bite of his double cheeseburger with triple bacon. The man sure knew how to eat, yet there didn't appear to be an ounce of fat on his muscular frame.

He was easy on the eyes. Goodness, who was she kidding? He was downright handsome, with his short military hair growing out and his tanned skin setting off his luscious chocolate eyes. And to top it off, he really listened when people spoke and was the most earnest person she'd ever met.

She shook off her attraction to Wyatt. "Nope. And if the new owner wants any rent, we're probably done because I'm still paying off my startup expenses."

"Those brand-new kennels must have cost a fortune. Especially the fancy ones that look like pieces of furniture."

She gazed into his face. Was he judging her for the

amount of money it cost to start her business? "I got them off of Facebook Marketplace for a steal. Some guy had planned to start a dog boarding business, but then he landed another corporate job, so it never happened. I bought the kennels from his wife, who shared with me that he had gotten sidetracked, which he often did. Those kennels were cheaper than used ones from any other place I searched because the lady was eager to clear out her garage and had no idea of the crates' value."

Surprise covered his features as he seemed taken aback by her fiery monologue.

Oops, she shouldn't have taken his comment so personally. Sometimes things were so black and white to her. She needed to focus on the reason they were here, to celebrate Harper. "I'm so excited about our girl," Autumn stated, then grinned.

Wait, had she said *our girl*? Oh no. That was wrong. She should have said *your girl*. Or maybe Harper.

Heat flamed Autumn's cheeks at her blunder.

His warm smile reached up to his crinkled eyes, as though he hadn't noticed her goof, and helped her get over her brief embarrassment. "Same here. Thanks for joining us tonight."

She almost hadn't come, but she was glad she'd pushed through. Being with Harper was making her believe she might have a chance at being a mom. Maybe a good one.

The server cleared the food from their table, and Harper ordered her coveted sundae.

"I loved sitting in the McCaw pew yesterday at church, Miss Autumn." Harper leaned her little head against Autumn's upper arm.

She gave the girl a tight hug, no longer surprised at the girl's comment about wanting a mommy like her. Harper likely meant nothing by it. Possibly said that to every maternal figure she met. "We enjoyed having you and your dad join us."

"Can I have my dolly?" she asked her father. Wyatt passed the bag to her.

But the mention of her tight-knit family, and the pregnancy and miscarriage that she'd withheld from them hovered in the air around her. Then guilt and remorse joined in to the party.

Autumn's family had trusted her, and she'd broken that trust. Telling the truth had been festering ever since she told Wyatt about the event. God had been pricking her heart to tell her loved ones about her past so their relationships could heal.

Except verbalizing the miscarriage to her family would infer an unwed pregnancy. Even today, shame twisted her insides over the actions that had caused her situation. If she told her family about her past, would they still love and accept her?

She'd had the perfect opportunity a week ago in her mother's kitchen, but she'd backed out.

Did she have the strength to come clean and deal with any potential fallout?

The secret was eating her up, even more so lately. She rubbed her damp hands on her slacks. She wished she had the courage to confess to her mother. Autumn figured if she could tell her mother, then the rest of the family would be easier to inform.

It was just the confession to her mother that tied her up in knots.

"Hey," Wyatt said, bringing her out of her troubling thoughts. "You okay?" He reached across the table and covered her hand with his massive one, then squeezed.

Her heart raced at the contact, but she didn't withdraw

her hand. It was comforting to have a partner by her side, for her business, of course. She savored the moment because she knew it couldn't last.

There was no way she would spoil her chance at success by becoming involved with her most important employee.

This relationship, or whatever was building between them, was a dead end.

Chapter Seven

A week later, gravel crunched in the lot near her mother's house. Autumn put Luna in her crate with a little treat for being so good and then peeked out to see who had arrived. Wyatt stepped out of his truck and butterflies fluttered in her stomach. When he looked her way with a wave, the butterflies took flight. He sported a well-worn pair of dark-wash jeans, grungy cowboy boots and a sky blue polo shirt with the Mighty Paws insignia on the right pocket that highlighted his broad biceps.

Baby raced down the incline and jumped at Wyatt's knees. He lifted the dog and let her lick his neck and cheeks before placing her on the ground.

He gazed up at her and gave her a crooked smile. Her cheeks flushed. She was surprised at her reaction. It had been over two weeks since she'd spilled her guts and told Wyatt everything. At first, their exchanges had taken a nosedive, with neither one knowing how to act with the other. Thankfully, their relationship had evened out, and they had begun a friendship, but she didn't expect more. Frankly, she didn't want more.

His smile turned into a grin as he climbed the incline. "You having a good Wednesday?"

"Couldn't be better," she said, pushing the unwelcome

feelings away. With her new business flourishing, she didn't need the complication of whatever was happening between them. "What are you doing home so early? And without Harper?" Had she really said *home*? That sounded so domestic.

She couldn't get over how attracted she'd become. Not just his good looks, but how he treated Harper and his work ethic drew her in as well.

"There were some cancellations, and the receptionist was able to work everyone into the morning slots so Doc Earl sent me home. Since Harper has been doing so well, I didn't want to mess with her routine so I decided to come back here to train dogs."

She gave a little clap. "Tallulah or Winston?"

"Buster." His smile disappeared, and something that looked like worry covered his features.

She tried to ignore his concerned look. "But he has a later promised date than the others."

"I think we need to work with Buster."

She brightened at his use of the word *we*. She liked that they had turned into a team. When he'd shown up on her doorstep a month ago and all the memories had rushed back to drown her, she never thought she'd be excited to see him. That she'd enjoy teaming up with him. But she really had.

He grabbed his sleeveless jacket with pockets full of treats and a red service vest for the dog, then headed for the training area while she fetched Buster, the adorable border collie they were training to be an allergy detection dog for a child with severe nut allergies.

As she walked out of the barn, she mulled over Wyatt's words. Was he worried about Buster's progress? She took in the happy tricolored dog as Wyatt replaced Buster's harness with the red service vest.

The dog immediately jumped on the platform. Wyatt released him and gave him a treat.

She freed a worried sigh. See, Buster was going to be fine.

Just then, Baby ran over and barked, capturing Buster's attention. The collie rushed over to Baby and started roughhousing with her. With his red vest on.

Her eyes widened. Wyatt had told Autumn the dogs would understand they were working when they had the official vest on. What was happening?

"Buster," Wyatt snapped.

The dog raced back to Wyatt, got a treat and immediately returned to Baby and their play.

"See?" he said.

His one-syllable word was loaded. She'd been afraid of this. Debra, her client, would be furious if Buster failed his training. "Maybe he's having an off day."

Wyatt slid her an annoyed glance and then continued vying with Baby for Buster's attention.

"I've also noticed Buster gets distracted easily, but I thought he'd grow out of it," she said. Now Wyatt's concerned look earlier made sense. "He's barely a year old."

"Remember what you told me the first day? More service dogs are released from training programs for socialization concerns than for any other reason." He quoted her. "I don't think Buster is making the cut."

"Let me put Baby up, then he'll give you his full attention."

But the defeated look on Wyatt's face matched what she'd been uneasy about for a while now.

"No, we have hard deadlines on Tallulah and Winston that we might meet." Wyatt swapped Buster's service vest for his harness. "Let's switch to Tallulah."

Autumn returned Buster to his crate, then grabbed one of the tiny Ziploc baggies holding a frozen cotton ball they'd gotten from Barbara with Tanner's saliva, taken when his blood sugar was low. She dropped the frozen cotton into a small, aluminum container with tiny holes in the top so the dog would catch the scent. Then she stuffed the baggie into a small metal garbage container with a lid that Wyatt had hung on the wall so none of the dogs would smell the trigger odors. Finally, she clipped the leash on Tallulah, excited that the Portuguese water dog's training was going well.

Wyatt started his training with basics, but quickly moved to the empty containers. As Tallulah was in a down stay on the platform, he placed the containers in a row, deftly slipping the scent box in the center block.

Since Tallulah wasn't a pro at this yet, he clipped a leash on her so he could lead her to each container to sniff. Very quickly, he guided her from block to block, using his hand to indicate that she should sniff and then follow him. At the odor-filled block she alerted. He said *down*, she lay down. He said *free* and Wyatt slipped her a reward. It all happened in a rush, apparently the dog needed to be moving quickly when actively working.

It took everything in Autumn not to cheer every time Tallulah alerted at the odor, but she refrained.

He placed Tallulah in a down stay on the platform, moved the odor block to a different position and tried again. She did a great job. He repeated it a number of times.

"Now, let's try getting her to remain down as I keep moving down the line of blocks," he said.

When she sniffed the odor she lay down, but as Wyatt kept moving, the dog followed so she didn't receive a treat. They started over and she got it right. They did it a few more times with about a 50 percent success rate.

"Pretty good for her first time," he said as he took off her service vest.

Autumn placed Tallulah in a pen so she could play with the other dogs. "What are we going to do about Buster?"

"I think we need to find another rescue dog to replace him and start the training process over."

Her heart dropped. Destiny would be devastated because she'd come to love Buster. Then Autumn thought of the little girl's mother, who was on the town council.

"Do you think Debra will understand that Buster has washed out?" she asked.

"Some service dogs fail. We'll explain it as best we can." He shrugged.

A niggle of worry crept into Autumn's head that she couldn't shake. Debra was a powerful woman who frankly scared Autumn. She was sharp and to the point and usually aired her grievances in public. Autumn was always thankful she wasn't her target when the woman went on a rant. Hopefully, she'd accept that Autumn wouldn't meet her original deadline and not overreact.

Wyatt touched her elbow. "Hey, your client will understand. Meeting two out of three dog-in-home target dates is going to be pretty amazing."

She took in his mesmerizing brown eyes with flecks of caramel and saw such support and enthusiasm for her business. She appreciated how they'd gotten to a place where they were working as a team. And finally, communicating with each other.

He blinked and his piercing gaze sucked her right in. She looked away. If she wasn't sure before, she was positive now—her romantic feelings toward Wyatt were real and growing, and they scared her.

Except, the last thing she wanted was a romance of any kind.

* * *

Later that evening, Autumn glanced at the door, hoping Harper's day had gone well. Oh, who was she kidding. She couldn't wait to see handsome Wyatt, which was crazy because they had spent the afternoon together. The question on the tip of her tongue, about Harper's time at day care, was just an excuse to initiate a conversation with him. She attempted to push away her thoughts of the engaging man, but they kept sneaking their way in.

In her parents' kitchen, pots and pans clanged as the last-minute preparations for dinner were underway. She dried a stockpot that her mother had boiled the potatoes in and put it away. The aroma of her mother's luscious pot roast tickled her nose, with a hint of cinnamon and sugar making Autumn hope for an apple pie for dessert.

Trisha, her sister-in-law, took items from Autumn's mother and slid them onto the island, readying the food for the weekly sit-down dinner.

Autumn still couldn't believe her mother had invited Wyatt to their Wednesday night family dinner. Thankfully, she and Wyatt had stopped discussing her prior pregnancy and now had an enjoyable working connection.

Her mother had always been curious why Autumn had stayed in Dallas so much longer than she had originally planned. Then, when she'd come home, she'd been so broken. Not just confused about what to do with her life—that was Autumn's usual state—but shattered. Thankfully, her mother had said nothing, though Autumn had seen the questions on her face. She'd not been honest with her mother and hated the distance that had grown between them.

During that time, Baby had been a calming force in her chaotic storm. She had started relying on her terrier to center her when memories plagued and wondered if God had placed Baby in her path. Prompted her to adopt the dog that fateful day.

Either way, she was grateful for the adorable terrier.

When Wyatt and Harper walked in, her heart somersaulted at his dressed-up jeans and checked chambray shirt. She gave him a courteous smile while his girl barreled across the kitchen. When Autumn caught her, her throat tightened with emotion at her growing feelings for this tyke. She twirled Harper around, relishing the giggles she got in return.

Baby raced in to greet Harper with a bark and an energetic tail wag. Harper crouched low to accept doggy kisses before the terrier pressed her nose against Autumn's leg and then raced to the other room.

Harper's words while they were walking to the diner about wanting a mother like Autumn had reignited her desire for motherhood, but she discarded the fanciful thought. She'd never be a mother, and the sooner she ridded herself of that hope, the better off she'd be. She focused on Harper and asked about her day. She said it was good, while looking longingly over Autumn's shoulder at the other kids playing. Autumn gave her one last squeeze and the girl rushed into the family room to play with Tori and Zoe, Laney and Ethan's twins.

"How's Harper faring in day care, Wyatt?" her mother asked.

"She's gone eight days now without needing to be picked up." He grinned and then glanced at Autumn.

As their gazes locked, warmth unfurled in her chest. She looked away.

Stop that. You guys had your chance. Anyway, you're too broken for him. For any man.

Except, the celebration meal at the diner a week and a

half ago had seemed to turn a switch between them. Since then, most evenings when she left the dog barn after settling the dogs for the night, she'd find Wyatt perched on the bottom step of the stairway leading to his apartment, as though waiting for her. At first he'd said he was getting some fresh air, but he could have done that on his landing. So she'd leaned against the railing and they'd discussed their days. Some nights their discussions traveled down the road of *remember when*, because their brief time together had been fun and their connection real. During the past few nights, their relationship had gone from awkward to cordial, and maybe more. Every day since, their communications had gotten easier, almost second nature. For the success of her business, that pleased her.

Laney entered the kitchen, carrying her sweet baby boy, and greeted Wyatt. "You two make a great team. The town is all abuzz about your training business now that Wyatt is on board." She graced Autumn with a wide grin.

Autumn's cheeks heated with the praise. Was there more to her relationship with Wyatt than just the dog training? She peeked at Wyatt, who was focused on the food spread out on the island. No. They'd both had their reasons for not entering a relationship back then and nothing had changed.

"Dinner is ready," her mother stated.

Everyone gathered around the island and brought a serving bowl or platter of hot food with them, set the steaming dishes in the center of the table and then took a seat.

Somehow Autumn ended up between Wyatt and Harper. She was close enough to touch the man. Smell his masculine scent. See the five-o'clock shadow on his chin.

Man, he was a good-looking.

"I hear Henry Wright has an interested buyer," Laney informed the settling group.

Autumn's head jerked up and caught her sister-in-law's gaze. No! She had been hoping it'd take a few years for Henry to hook a buyer. Or maybe he'd have a change of heart and decide to remain in Serenity, where his only grandkids lived.

Baby, stationed at Autumn's feet, pushed her nose against her owner's thigh and whined. Autumn dropped her hand and scratched the top of the terrier's head.

"Let's pray, then we can eat," her father responded.

But all Autumn could think about was her dog training and boarding business. She'd go under without Henry's barn. She had no other leasing options.

For a year now she'd adjusted her life to focus on this business, especially training dogs to couple them with children in need. What would she do if she lost her training facility?

Right then a large hand patted her knee twice and then disappeared.

She flashed a look at Wyatt, who winked at her. Her heart pitter-pattered at the kind gesture.

She laced her fingers together in her lap because her first inclination was to reach for his hand.

Though she was grateful for his encouragement, she wasn't so sure she wanted them to be anything other than employee and employer.

Between possibly losing her leased business space and her burdensome secret, Autumn didn't have the bandwidth to consider more than friendship with Wyatt. But the more time they spent together, the more intrigued she became about the possibility.

Wyatt was thankful and overwhelmed at being included in the McCaw Wednesday night family dinner.

He bowed his head as Autumn's father prayed over the meal, proceeding to thank God for bringing the blessing of Wyatt to Autumn.

As soon as grace was over, the serving platters and bowls moved around the table at warp speed. Meat and potatoes and gravy. His stomach growled at the enticing scents. These people knew how to eat—he liked that.

He turned Wade's words of him being a blessing over in his head. He sure didn't feel like a blessing. Part of him wished he'd chosen to relocate somewhere else because he'd clearly brought emotions back to Autumn that she hadn't dealt with and didn't want to deal with.

But maybe this was all in God's plan, since Serenity was his grandmother's home and his mother had moved here to take care of Nana.

He spared a glance at Autumn, sitting next to him, her drawn features screamed she was worried about Henry having a buyer. She was adorable when she was worried.

Enough. She is only a friend.

"Where'd you hear that Henry has a buyer?" Autumn asked Laney.

"Esther, Doc Earl's wife, told me when I was in the consignment shop earlier."

Autumn nodded and then rolled her head as if to loosen up tight muscles brought on by stress.

The situation concerned him as well. Not only did he love training dogs and adore the apartment he received in exchange for training, but he had caught Autumn's vision and now the urge to train service dogs for her eager clients was driving him every day. What had happened seven years ago no longer colored his feelings when Autumn came to mind. Instead, he focused on the person she had become and the noble service dog dream she pursued.

With each day that passed, he and Autumn seemed to grow closer. He looked forward to their chats after Harper was settled for the night. Maybe more than he should. They'd turned into the highlight of his day.

"Even if Henry has a buyer, that doesn't mean Autumn can't keep using the dog barn," he said.

When Autumn looked up at him as though his opinion mattered, his heart picked up speed.

Yes, she was gorgeous on the outside, but the more he came to know her and learn about her passion for getting trained dogs into the hands of people in need, the stronger his attraction grew.

When they'd first reconnected and he'd seen those shiny new crates, especially the swanky furniture type ones, he'd assumed she was a spender, like his ex-wife. But the other night at the diner, when he discovered she'd gotten them at a deep discount, he realized he was wrong about Autumn. She was nothing like his ex-wife. Autumn didn't believe money could buy happiness.

"We're glad you and Harper could make it tonight," Cora, Autumn's mother, stated, a wide smile on her lips.

Last week he'd immediately declined her invite because he'd still felt funny about Autumn having gone through a difficult miscarriage because of him. But now he felt like he and Autumn were friends, and the past was where it belonged.

"We're happy to be here." And he was. As a kid, he'd longed for a family like this, but his father had been a liar and a cheat. His father's actions had molded Wyatt. Taught him not to trust. But he hoped he was recovering from those wounds.

Harper, sitting beside her new best friend, Autumn, kept her head down as she took small bites of the baby carrots.

He knew she loved playing with Tori and Zoe, but in this large crowd of people she was acting a bit shy and he didn't blame her. The McCaw clan was noisy and loud, but clearly full of love and acceptance.

A cool dog nose bumped his leg. He looked down. Baby sat between him and Autumn, though she wasn't begging or expecting food like a dog usually would at the dinner table. It was almost as if she was standing at attention in case she was needed.

He loved how Autumn had the necessary support, not only with Baby but with her loving family.

Though he enjoyed spending time with her, he found her laugh, her funny jokes, her passion for the dogs and her mere presence distracted him when they were together. And that kind of scared him.

"Potatoes?" Walker asked.

Wyatt picked up the bowl and passed it to Autumn's brother, who gave him a kind look as a thank you.

So much laughter, so many smiles and cheerful faces. Could they really be this joyful? Part of Wyatt was skeptical about all this kindness around the table, but a larger part of him hoped the McCaws were genuine and that families really were this happy.

Harper giggled. "You're funny," she told Wade.

His daughter seemed so happy, like a light switch had gone off with whatever dad joke Wade had just made.

Autumn smiled at him, as if to confirm that Harper could handle this crowd. He appreciated how deeply Autumn cared for his daughter.

Wyatt and Autumn had fallen into a comfortable rhythm of working together, and Harper loved living at the Triple C.

He and Harper spent so much of their free time at the dog barn and Autumn was always there. Yes, she owned the business, but sometimes he couldn't think straight when he was with her.

"I hear Tallulah is going to camp with Tanner in July. That is so exciting," Cora stated.

Autumn lifted her chin and gazed at her mother. "Actually, we're not going to hit the July first date with Tallulah. Though she's great, Wyatt still has a good bit of training to make her a successful scent-related service dog." She shot a warm smile his way. "He also needs to work with Tanner so the two can be a successful team."

The moment their gazes connected, his pulse sped up.

Wyatt breathed a sigh of relief that Autumn was no longer upset with him for going behind her back to speak with Tanner's mom.

"But we'll only be off by a week or so," he said. And he was hoping that'd still give him enough time with Tanner so the boy could attend camp.

Autumn jumped in to give an update on Winston. As she finished talking with her mother, he studied Autumn's profile. Her high cheekbones highlighted her moss green eyes that sparkled whenever she was discussing dogs. Tonight, her honey-blond hair hung in waves down her back, similar to how it looked at the diner over a week ago, at Harper's celebratory dinner.

Autumn made some type of joke that he hadn't heard, and she bumped him with her shoulder. Warmth threaded through him at the touch.

"You two are so cute, you'd make a good couple," Laney said and then leaned over to cut Zoe's meat with a grin on her face.

Wyatt stilled.

No, that would not happen. Chloe had taught him a valuable lesson—relationships don't work. He'd learned that as a kid watching his parent's train wreck of a marriage. And Chloe had added the exclamation point. No matter how well he and Autumn got along, they could never be more than friends.

Harper sighed and then looked up at Laney with a grin. "Daddy and Miss Autumn were in love a long time ago." She turned to Autumn. "Don't people in love get married? Daddy and I went to Noah and Emily's wedding because they were in love. That was fun."

Wyatt's throat seized up at his daughter sharing that personal tidbit she must have overheard when he and Autumn were talking in the dog barn about dating.

Conversation ground to a halt as all eyes focused on Autumn.

He hadn't been there for Autumn seven years ago, but he was here today and he'd do whatever he could to support her.

Except the looks on her family's faces were judgmental, not compassionate, which disappointed Wyatt. He thought the McCaws might be different.

No wonder Autumn was afraid to tell her family the truth.

Chapter Eight

Scenery passed by in a blur as Wyatt and Autumn headed to a rescue to look at a few potential service dogs. He glanced at Autumn. In the passenger seat of his truck, she stared straight ahead and appeared anxious as she held Baby on her lap.

"Sorry about Harper's offhand comment," he said. Last night, his stomach had dropped when the conversation had ground to a halt and all eyes focused on Autumn.

The truck hit a pothole, and Autumn reached for the dashboard to steady herself and the terrier.

"It's not your fault," she replied. "Apparently she over-heard us." She pressed a kiss to the top of Baby's head.

She was wrong. It was all his fault. Harper had amazing hearing, and he should have taken that into account as they spoke. Last night, when Harper made her statement, Wyatt realized just how much he cared for Autumn. Way more than he was comfortable with.

He was a born fixer, and the fact that he couldn't fix this situation was driving him crazy. He'd missed an important phone call seven years ago that changed the course of Autumn's life, and clearly she was still wounded by the situation.

"I'm glad Harper's doing so well at day care."

His lips spread into a satisfied smile. "Agreed. I've gotten a few calls since the first day she made it through, but the director has put Harper on the phone and we talk for a few minutes, and then she seems fine. The director believes she may be afraid of losing me."

It had been almost two weeks since the celebratory dinner at the diner where his relationship with Autumn had undergone a sudden change. The effort to keep it all business had disappeared and the attraction had grown.

As the truck rumbled along, he breathed deeply and savored the heady scent of Autumn's barely there floral perfume. He'd become accustomed to being with her and was beginning to enjoy their time together.

It had taken him almost a month to process what Autumn had told him. Because he'd needed a voice of reason, he'd told his mother what had transpired, including the pregnancy, miscarriage and missed phone calls. She'd been unhappy with his actions but helped him realize he couldn't change the past.

She'd told him to let the misunderstanding about the phone calls go. Those discussions had helped him move past the horror that he hadn't been there for her and now he was trying to live in the present.

Autumn's phone dinged. She jostled Baby so she could read the message. "Ugh. Teresa, the rescue dog lady, had something come up. She wants to push the meet and greet back an hour."

He slowed the truck as his pulse kicked up a notch at spending an hour with Autumn.

"Tell her that works just fine. I don't need to get Harper from day care since my mother's going to pick her up and feed her dinner."

Autumn's thumbs flew over her phone. "What do you want to do? We already had lunch."

"We passed a park a few miles back. Maybe we can find a trail and take a little hike?" He took a left, intending to head back to where they'd come from.

"Baby would love that."

He pulled into the park and immediately spotted a one-mile hike. The trail was wide, so there was ample room to hike side by side. Decision made, he parked and they exited the vehicle.

They made their way to the path with Baby on the other side of Autumn. They were walking as close as possible without holding hands. Autumn looked gorgeous in a denim jumpsuit that flared at her knees, and she'd traded her worn cowboy boots for little white sneakers. It was as if she'd dressed up to visit rescue dogs, including adding that irresistible perfume. The sun glinted off her hair, which was curly today, as she flashed a smile at him. Had she dressed up for him or the rescue dogs? He liked to think it was for him.

"What do you think the director means by Harper being afraid of losing you?" Autumn's voice was tentative, as though she wasn't sure he'd want to share with her.

But his past needed to be stated out loud. He'd relied on his mother long enough. He needed to open his sphere of trusted confidantes, at least a little.

A squirrel skittered in front of them, and Baby lunged toward it, her leash stopping her from the chase. When the squirrel disappeared, Baby calmed down, but her ears were now perked.

"After my wife left, the next two years were a roller coaster, since Chloe kept dropping in wanting to visit with Harper. She had serious drug issues, but each time I let her take Harper, she was clean, or so she said." He pushed a branch out of his way and held it for Autumn to pass by. "I mean, no matter what had happened between us, I wanted Harper to have a relationship with her mother." His throat tightened with emotion, remembering their past.

"That's so hard." Her tender expression made him dizzy.

The trees cocooned them in with each step they took. With no other hikers in sight, Wyatt focused on the trail and pushed his emotions away so he could continue explaining.

"Each time Harper came home, she'd have difficulty sleeping for a few nights." His daughter's turmoil had turned him inside out. "I should have figured it out, but I so wanted her to have a normal childhood, or as close to normal as possible."

"I can understand the desire to give Harper both parents, but wasn't it obvious your wife was using?"

"Not really. Apparently she had become good at lying, something I'd never seen in her before." The path narrowed, and he slowed to allow Autumn and Baby to pass in front of him. "I tried to be cautious each time Chloe took Harper, but about six months ago, when Harper was visiting her mother, I woke up to the police knocking on my door in the middle of the night with my daughter, because Chloe had been part of a drug sting."

Autumn stopped, and her fingers flew to her lips in horror. "No."

"I felt horrible. So responsible." In fact, he had blamed God for not giving him some type of signal to keep his daughter safe.

His mother's advice about relying on God and surrendering to Him came to mind. Except, seeing his daughter in pain was hard. He hoped Harper's healing process would allow her to emerge stronger from the incident. But what parent wants their child to go through such panic and fear? Not him, that's for sure.

But as the days and weeks had passed, he'd realized God wasn't at fault. It had been Chloe and her poor choices.

"I'm so sorry you and Harper went through that. It sounds awful." A lock of hair blew across her face. His fingers itched to tuck it back into place, but he restrained himself as they continued on the path.

He'd never shared that story with anyone other than his mother and Nana. Frankly, saying it out loud made him realize he'd been giving God more blame than was necessary. A shot of remorse traveled to his chest. With this fresh start, including a new church and pastor, he should work out his issues with God before they festered too deeply into his brain and messed up Harper's relationship with the Lord.

He sucked in a breath of fresh air as Autumn and Baby picked their way through the root-laden path. It felt good to lighten the burden by sharing the story with a friend, and he knew his past was safe with her.

"You're a good father, Wyatt. Never question that." She placed her petite hand on his upper arm and he stopped.

"I made decisions to let Harper be with her mother and goodness knows what *might have* happened." The fear was real. He'd never forget the moment he opened the door to the police, the female officer holding a sobbing Harper.

Autumn's fingers tightened around his biceps, and without thinking, his hand covered hers. "No," she said. "Don't do that to yourself. Harper's safe now."

His gaze moved from the longing in her shimmering eyes, then traced the shape of her face, moving from the wispy pieces of hair near her cheeks down to her parted lips. They were standing so close to each other. What would she do if he kissed her?

His pulse kicked up a notch as he licked his lips and moved toward her. But then he heard noises in the distance, someone talking. He paused, wanting to kiss her but not wanting to be interrupted in such a monumental moment. As the voices grew louder, Baby yipped and lunged toward the unseen hikers, so he stepped away with a groan on his lips.

He rubbed a hand over his hair, finally growing out from the short military style he'd worn for so long, as his pulse returned to a normal range.

The nervousness now covering Autumn's face made him grateful for the interruption. A romance would mess up the equilibrium they had reached, and he liked their new normal. He hadn't thought through the ramifications of kissing his boss and his daughter's new best friend.

He took another step away as the chatty hikers neared.

No, it'd be much safer if they remained friends and only friends.

Frankly, she probably wasn't interested in a man with his track record. Even if she could look past his failed marriage, he couldn't. Autumn deserved better than him.

After their awkward almost-kiss, they adopted three adorable and solid dogs that would become Autumn's second round of scent-related service animals. On their return trip, Wyatt had asked if she wanted to work with Tallulah and Winston when they got back. Yes, absolutely.

She was astonished Wyatt had shared so much of his heart on their walk. All the yucky stuff about his ex-wife. How he had tried to keep a relationship going between Harper and Chloe, even after his ex had abandoned them. But what really made her speechless was his willingness to give up his life and career to create distance from Chloe after the drug bust had wounded Harper. He was such an amazing father and protector.

When they returned to the Triple C, Wyatt asked, "It might rain later on. Would you mind if I move the platform into the barn? I was thinking of leaning it against the wall opposite the crates." She agreed.

While he did that, she let the new dogs into a pen to run and sniff. They seemed friendly with one another, but she'd have to be careful introducing them to the others. She settled on a hay bale to observe their personalities, but her mind was still reeling from her time with Wyatt. His admission of his past marriage woes and the horrors little Harper had endured tugged at her heart. But mostly the memory of their electric moment sizzled in her mind.

Wyatt joined her. "They look like they are pretty calm," he said, referring to their recent additions. She nodded, itching to get some more training done. He put a palm on her leg. "I'm really sorry Harper said that last night."

She gazed into his chocolate brown eyes that sparkled with interest just like earlier during the almost-kiss, and she scooted away. "Not a problem." Though it was a problem because, last night, she'd seen the knowing look her mother gave her after Harper's comment. She was going to have to come clean to her mother sooner versus later. The guilt was eating her up. She stood and fetched Tallulah, while Wyatt gathered the cinder blocks he would use in the training session.

She'd been shocked at the almost-kiss, but was glad it hadn't happened. Kind of. Her feelings this time around were much different. Not only were they both Christians, but her affections for Wyatt now ran deep. Much deeper than she preferred.

But their working relationship had hit a good stride.

Anyway, he was her employee, so maybe they'd best keep things in the friend zone. Regardless, she had this secret she'd been keeping from her family and felt about to burst if she didn't reveal it. Especially since Harper had made her little announcement.

After she put Tallulah's red vest on, she placed the pup in a down stay and went to the big dog pen. She lifted a wriggling Baby out and pulled her close to her chest for comfort. She breathed in the dog's soothing smell and settled on a different hay bale perch where she could see Wyatt train Tallulah.

"Thanks," Wyatt said as he pointed at a now quivering Tallulah, all excited about getting to work again.

She nodded and settled Baby on her lap so she could watch the training.

He'd set up seven cinder blocks wrapped in duct tape, just like he'd done the other day. They practiced a few times with no scent, making sure Tallulah remembered to investigate each one presented to her.

He then put the scent in the center block, and though Tallulah alerted on the odor, she continued to follow Wyatt down the row, so she didn't receive a treat. She was supposed to stay with the scent. He repeated the process and Tallulah had learned her mistake and remained at the scented block the next few times. Autumn was elated by Tallulah's learning and by Wyatt's masterful training. It didn't hurt that Wyatt was easy on the eyes. In fact, he was probably the handsomest man she'd ever met.

"She's doing so good, isn't she, Baby?" Autumn wrapped her arms around her companion's shoulders and gently squeezed. "I'm so excited about how well the service dogs are doing." The terrier swiped Autumn's chin in response.

Then Wyatt moved the scent block to different positions in the row of containers, and Tallulah did great with each try.

"How do you know she's not watching and memorizing where you're putting the scent block?"

He graced Autumn with a wide smile, reminding her that the worry he'd arrived at the Triple C with over a month ago seemed to be completely gone. She wasn't sure if it was because he was hours away from his disaster of an ex-wife or his new job or how well Harper had adjusted to life in Serenity, but she was thrilled to see him so happy.

"Good reminder," he said as he settled the scent block into a new position. "I'll pretend like I'm putting a treat in each one, just in case she's as smart as you think." He reached into his pocket and then placed his empty hand in the first cinder block, as though dropping a treat in, and repeated the process for each of them.

They did a couple more tries and Tallulah alerted on the scent each time.

"Now I'm going to elevate all the blocks."

He placed the mostly black dog in a down stay near the pens, but the pup didn't pay any attention to the barking and whining dogs near her. She was focused solely on Wyatt, who went into the barn and returned with the platform.

"I didn't think Tallulah would progress to an elevated surface today." He put the platform down and placed the blocks sideways so they'd be right at nose level for the dog.

Wyatt released the dog with his search command, then moved to each block, presenting it with his hand while Tallulah sniffed each one until she alerted on the scent. Wyatt released the dog with his free command and treated her. They repeated it a few times.

Maybe Wyatt had spoken with Barbara too quickly. Seemed like Tallulah was on the fast track. Autumn could only hope they'd meet her dog-in-home deadline, then Tanner could go to camp.

"Good dog," Wyatt said as he crouched and scratched the top of the Portuguese water dog's head and removed her red vest. "Next time, we'll try it with different containers to mix it up a bit."

They repeated the exercise with Winston, who didn't catch on as quickly. He kept tripping up on not waiting for the free command after he alerted as well as following Wyatt after he had smelled the scent.

"Should I be worried?" she asked.

He chuckled. "No. Each dog learns at their own pace. Like Tallulah just got it." He snapped his fingers. "Winston will too, but just not today." He took the dog's vest off and placed him in the pen so he could play with his friends.

Autumn gave Baby one last snuggle and then dropped her back into the big dog pen. Baby preened around as the dogs sniffed her, likely wondering why she always got special treatment.

"Have you heard anything from Henry?" he asked.

"Crickets." She'd shot him a text after dinner last night asking if he knew anything about the buyer, like if the new owner would let her use the barn rent-free.

"I don't know what I'm going to do if I can't keep using this barn."

Wyatt took her hand and squeezed. "It'll work out. I know you don't think there is anywhere else you could have this business, but we'll make it work. I'm confident."

The warmth of his hand felt good. But even better was his oath to help her succeed.

She leaned her head against his sturdy shoulder and thanked him.

She'd started this business two years ago by looking

for a location to house her dogs, and the barn on the edge of Henry's property had been her only option. Real estate hadn't changed in the past two years.

So even though it felt good to hold his hand and lean against his strong and capable shoulder, *she* was the owner of this business. He had a full-time job and a life outside of her boarding and training business. If her venture collapsed, he'd go on his merry way.

And she'd once again be labeled as a failure by her family, her church community and everyone else in Serenity. She didn't think she could handle that again.

Chapter Nine

The next day, Autumn stood rooted in the peaceful entrance of her dog barn and eyed her parents' house. The cloudy day matched her gloomy mood because today was the day. Today she planned to spill her shameful secret to her mother. Would she judge Autumn and look down on her? Be upset she hadn't come to her for moral support?

All her mother knew was that she had gone to Dallas for a probable career move and returned two years later a changed woman. Her mother had assumed the changed part was her spiritual walk. What she didn't know was what had precipitated her need for God's strength in her life.

She pressed a kiss to Baby's forehead. "I couldn't do this without you." She gazed into her terrier's eyes, so thankful Baby had helped her for so many years. Determined to do this alone, she placed her canine companion on the ground.

She put one step in front of the other, gravel crunching under her worn cowboy boots. Maybe after this talk, she'd be able to move forward in her life and truly put the past behind her. Because telling Wyatt had begun to heal her heart, and maybe, just maybe, this next conversation would help as much.

The fixed landing, enclosing the entrance to Wyatt's garage apartment, caught her eye. A couple of days ago, he had put two gently used lawn chairs in the tiny space. That first evening, after he put Harper down for bed, he'd called to Autumn as she was leaving the dog barn. Her heart flip-flopped with each step she took toward him. The landing was so small that the chairs kissed. As she settled against the weaves of the chair, she could smell soap indicating he'd washed away the grime of the day. He'd asked her about her day and almost immediately they'd fallen into a smooth rhythm of helping each other with their problems and encouraging one another.

Every evening since, they had spent hours chatting just as they previously had at the base of the steps. Wyatt's purchase of these chairs seemed significant. He genuinely appeared to enjoy their time together and wanted their nightly conversations to be comfortable. She'd been surprised at the amount they had in common. Surprised they'd been able to put the pregnancy and miscarriage in the rearview mirror.

Then last night he'd said something about how different she was now versus when they met on the island. Said her determination and drive impressed him. The crinkles around his tender brown eyes had drawn her in.

His compliment had warmed her, likely more than it should have. Her excitement over starting this business had come to life once she had seen what a service dog could do for a broken individual. Now her ambition thrived.

She opened her parents' back door and a sweet aroma drifted through the air. Her mother was probably baking something tasty. Seeing Wyatt a month ago had opened up a flood of emotions she had stuffed down and not dealt with.

"You home," she called out. Her chest squeezed at the upcoming conversation. Would her mother still love and respect her once she knew?

Her mother bustled over, wrapping Autumn in a warm hug. "I missed you this morning. You left rather early."

As she squeezed her mother back, grief seized her throat and caught Autumn off guard. The miscarriage felt like yesterday, not almost a decade ago. She choked down a swallow and focused on her mother.

"Come, come, I'm making double chocolate chip cookies, your favorite. Let me pour you a coffee."

"No thanks," she said, following her mother into the kitchen. She actually felt like she was going to throw up. She just needed to get the confession over with.

"It's warm out today. How about some sweet tea? I know you love a cold glass of—"

"I have something to say," Autumn sharply interrupted her mother. "And I need to say it now."

Her mother stilled, then slipped into her kitchen chair and slid her laptop to the side. Autumn remained standing. She wasn't sure her knees would bend to allow her to sit.

Haltingly, she told her mother of the pregnancy. Her throat grew dry, but the sympathy and love on her mother's face gave her the boldness to push through.

"At five months, the doctor couldn't find a heartbeat," her voice cracked.

She adored her family and didn't want to lose their trust and love. Her stomach was all knotted up, thinking about the possible fallout from this conversation.

Then she told her mother that to preserve the possibility of having children in the future, she'd had to deliver the baby. She had an uneasy feeling she would never forget the moment and that it would continue to define her for the rest of her days. Her mother's expression changed from sympathy to sadness.

"Sweetheart," her mother said as she stood, pulled Autumn close and enveloped her only daughter in a tight hug. "I'm so sorry you've dealt with this alone for so long."

Autumn wept in her mother's arms, as she had longed to years ago. The crying sapped her of energy.

"I'm proud of you," her mother whispered in her ear.

"*Proud* isn't the word I think of when I look back on that time in my life."

Her mother held her at arm's length. "You didn't take the easy way out, sweetheart, and you ended up going through a trying experience." Her voice held deep compassion. "When you returned from Dallas, I could see you were sad, but also a stronger person."

Autumn shook her head. Her mother had it all wrong. When she'd come home, clinging to Baby, she'd been so broken. Still was.

"No, I'm not stronger, not at all. I've been living in grief and shame for seven years." Her voice cracked when she uttered *shame*. Some days, she felt like the word was written on her heart. Like that was all God saw when he viewed her.

Her mother gathered her close again. "Oh, honey, I'm so sorry you went through that alone. I could have been there. I promise I wouldn't have judged."

She swallowed the lump that had formed in her throat and allowed the relief to sink in. "Thank you."

Her mother took her hands and squeezed them.

Gazing at her mother, Autumn realized the ache of carrying this burden alone was gone. She was thankful for her mother's kind reaction and loving support.

Her mother led her to the table and settled her in a chair, then fetched her a tall glass of sweet tea. Autumn took a long drink before meeting her mother's gaze again.

"You realize that time in your life doesn't define you, right?" her mother stated. "God sees you as a new creation in Christ. He doesn't see any past moral failures. You are clean in his eyes."

Autumn took in the scene around her and realized by the acceptance on her mother's face that the shame she'd chosen to carry all these years did not define her.

Was her mother right? Had God used her journey of pregnancy and miscarriage to draw her to Him? Could that have been the sole purpose of that time in her life?

"I assume the father wasn't involved?"

Autumn's cheeks flamed. This conversation would have been so much easier if her family didn't know Wyatt. He was an amazing man and the last thing she wanted was for them to hold that situation against him.

"No," she said. Then she informed her mother that Wyatt was the father of the baby and they'd been together briefly at an island resort. She then shared about the mix-up—that he'd used a disposable phone so she hadn't known his real phone number.

"It all makes sense now. You were looking for a dog trainer, but when the perfect trainer came along, you didn't seem excited about him at all." She touched Autumn's hand. "Wyatt arriving brought all the feelings you had suppressed to the forefront, didn't it?"

Autumn's chin trembled. "Yes, but I told him and we've moved past that."

A car door slammed. Was that Wyatt getting back from work and day care? Dread coursed through her at how she might have tainted her family against him.

Though Autumn felt so much better getting the truth off her chest, she hoped it didn't affect Wyatt's relationship with any of her family.

Her mother's eyes misted. "Now I know why you seem to keep loved ones at an arm's length."

She didn't want to be the person her mother described. Not anymore.

Now that everything was out in the open, she'd be better about having genuine conversations with family members.

Her mother drew her into another hug, this time more fierce. "That must have been so difficult to go through all alone." Her mother pulled back and placed her hands on Autumn's shoulders. "Well, you're not alone anymore, sweetheart."

She was stunned she'd been able to share everything she had kept locked inside for so long. The longer she had held it in, the worse she had felt.

Now she felt better. Drained, but much better.

Maybe she shouldn't have hidden the truth from her loved ones, because this had been a step in healing. Maybe, just maybe, she wasn't the failure she thought she was.

"This also explains why you haven't dated," her mother said and then patted Autumn's hand.

Surprise zinged around Autumn's head. She hadn't really thought about the reason why she hadn't dated.

"Want to help me put these cookies in the oven?" her mother asked. Autumn's stomach growled and they shared a carefree laugh.

They stood and walked to the kitchen hand in hand, her mother clearly showing her support for Autumn.

They washed their hands and then, side by side, they balled up cookie dough.

Autumn hadn't felt this free in seven years.

That horrible free fall feeling had ended. Replaced with peace.

Her mind conjured up handsome Wyatt. He always smelled faintly of soap and some pleasant earthy scent. His tanned arms were corded with muscles she couldn't take her eyes off. And his smile, every time he aimed his adorable crooked smile at her it made her giddy. Then last night, when his eyes had looked at her full of affection, she'd almost leaned across the metal arm of the lawn chair and kissed him.

"Thinking of Wyatt?"

Autumn's cheeks pinked. "Mom, no." She focused on the cookie dough.

Her mother lifted Autumn's chin with her index finger and made eye contact. "Sweetie, he seems like a great guy. Perhaps this is your second chance?"

Maybe her mother was right.

Because she no longer wanted to live in the past. She wanted to live life to the fullest.

Could she and Wyatt build their friendship into something more?

The sun was low in the sky as Wyatt kept his eyes trained on the dog barn. He'd put Harper to bed and perched on the little landing outside his apartment. Because he didn't want to be stuck in the living room every evening, he'd purchased two lawn chairs at the consignment store the other day.

He shook his head. Who was he kidding? He'd been enjoying the chats he and Autumn had been having at the base of the steps every evening and thought if he had seating on the landing maybe she'd stay longer. He could only hope.

In the distance, Autumn closed the dog barn door and headed to her parents' home, where she lived. She'd likely just finished making her final rounds with the dogs. His chest constricted at the sight of her.

"Autumn," he called.

She looked up at Wyatt and grinned, then headed for the steps that led to his landing, Baby on her heel.

His heart quickened as she neared. He found himself captivated by her. Enchanted by their discussions.

Whoa. What was he thinking? He was grateful their kiss had been interrupted, because he still clung to his belief that he couldn't trust others to stick around. Though, where was Autumn going? Other than her brief stint in Dallas, she'd lived in Serenity her whole life. Now she had a business to run.

She climbed the stairs and stepped onto his little landing. She then settled in the other chair, the one he'd purchased for her, while Baby curled up at her feet.

Maybe he could give a relationship with her a try? Maybe she'd be different.

"This is nice." Her sweet smile directed at him caused a sudden blip in his pulse. She pulled the clip from the back of her head and released her hair. Her dark blond mane cascaded onto her shoulders. She had no idea how gorgeous she was, even after a long day at work.

Get it together, man.

He leaned back against the chair webbing and fought his rising emotions.

"How was your day?" Could she hear the deep affection in his voice? He hoped not. But he really cared how her day had gone.

She closed her eyes for a moment, then turned to look at him. Pain and something like hope shimmered in their depths. "I told my mom everything." Baby jumped into her lap, circled twice and then curled into an exhausted ball.

His heart pinched with empathy for Autumn. That discussion must have been hard. "I'm proud of you for having the guts to tell your family and get it off your chest. We're not supposed to walk through life alone."

He wanted to reach over and pat her hand, give her the

encouragement she deserved, but he didn't. Would she welcome his touch or push him away? It didn't matter because right now she needed a listening ear.

"My mom asked, and I told her you were the father. I apologize in advance if my family is upset with you."

"You did the right thing. It was the truth." Once again, he kicked himself for not exchanging his Texas number with her.

When she lifted a finger and swiped away an errant tear, a vise tightened around his heart.

He'd put her in this situation. If they'd kept their encounter on the island pure, they wouldn't be having this conversation. One of the first things he'd learned after handing his life over to Christ was how men were called to act with integrity in relationships. He hadn't done that with Autumn. An ache expanded in his chest.

She let out a deep sigh. "Enough about that. How's your grandmother doing? Was the last treatment as bad as the first?"

He gave her a quick update, thankful that Nana seemed stronger, instead of weaker, after the last round of chemotherapy. Maybe it was having a quiet home to relax in.

"It's so nice that your mother moved here to care for her. I just love the multigenerational family thing." She pushed a lock of hair that had gotten entangled in her lips away. The movement made him focus on her kissable lips. Maybe he *wasn't* thankful for the hikers interrupting their moment the other day. "What about your father?" she asked. "You never talk about him."

He pulled his gaze from her face. This wasn't a topic he liked to discuss, but she had shared her secret with her mother and opened up so much to him. The least he could do was honor her question.

He roughed a palm over his face. "He left my mother," Wyatt spit out, still so mad with his dad. "He had been cheating on her. In fact, when I was a teen, I found him in a compromising position and my father misused my trust. It was horrible to know something like that and not be able to tell my mother."

His anger toward his father was palpable. Sometimes it felt like a person in the room with him. His mother had told him he needed to forgive so that he could let go of the past. But that was hard to do when his father had forced him into a no-win situation when he'd insisted Wyatt lie for him. Wyatt had been thirteen years old and wanted nothing more than his parents to remain married. So he'd done what he was told. But it hadn't taken long for his parents' marriage to fall apart. He always felt responsible for some of the pain his mother went through during that time.

As a fixer, Wyatt struggled with giving up control. He knew God could handle everything. He also knew that holding on to anger wasn't doing him and his daughter any good.

"I'm so sorry your father hurt you."

Something about Autumn made him want to share. Maybe even heal. He wanted to have a give-and-take exchange that mutually benefited them. But he had learned from the past that was impossible.

"I guess that's why, when my wife cheated on me and left me in debt, along with the horrors she ended up putting Harper through, I realized others will always abuse my trust."

"Oh, Wyatt, don't allow one person to define you."

He glanced at her. Why did she have such faith in people? "Love doesn't last forever because people are too selfish to commit," he informed her. "Love is only temporary. Like a vapor, it's here today and gone tomorrow."

Autumn shook her head. "No, Wyatt, that's not true. You can't go through life not trusting people. Keeping people at arm's length." Her slender fingers touched his forearm, warming his skin with her affection. "I should know. My mother accused me of the same thing earlier, and you know what? She was right. Anyway, that's not the example you want to give Harper, is it?"

Did he keep people at arm's length? If he were honest with himself, yes, he did. But that didn't affect his daughter, did it?

He kept people at a distance to safeguard his heart as well as Harper's, which was the right thing to do.

Autumn's fingertips pulsed against his skin. He'd planned to keep her at a distance, but look at what was happening. Did she feel the magnetic pull between them, too?

Maybe she was right. Maybe he pushed people away. She removed her hand to pet Baby's head.

That was when the light dawned on how he'd been living his life. Because of two people, he'd been pushing the rest of the world away and training his daughter to do the same.

He sure didn't want his daughter to end up a recluse like him.

Maybe now was the time to allow people in instead of forging down the path of isolation with his daughter. He wanted Harper to be a healthy grown-up one day.

And he wasn't just accepting help from Autumn, she was also indebted to him. Without Wyatt, she wouldn't be able to train service dogs. They had a mutually beneficial relationship, and he was learning to accept that.

"You might be right," he said.

With darkness enveloping them, he gazed at her. She

nibbled on her lower lip and groves deepened between her eyebrows. Was something wrong?

"Henry is having a hard time getting a straight answer from the buyer," she said, disappointment lacing her tone.

"I can't imagine the buyer will want to use your dog barn. It's just so far away from the house and other outbuildings on the property."

"Thanks, but I'm afraid my business is going to be short-lived if I don't come up with another way to infuse cash into the business. I need to be able to pay some rent to the new owner." She gripped the arms of the lawn chairs so tight her knuckles turned white. Baby lifted her head, but must not have thought Autumn needed her because she soon dropped it and emitted soft snores. "As it is, I barely make enough money to pay my measly bills. How can I pay *any* rent? I mean, the best I can hope for is that the buyer demands some type of rent in exchange for me using the dog barn. The worst is that he won't let me use the dog barn. Then what'll I do?"

"For starters, it's us, not you. We're in this together, Autumn. I see your vision and want to do anything I can to help this mission succeed."

She tipped her head to the side and gave him a half-hearted smile. "Thanks, Wyatt, that means a lot." She pressed back into the weave of the chair and her smile disappeared. When her shoulders drooped, it looked like she'd already lost the fight.

He straightened. She needed help, and he was always abuzz with ideas. If he did nothing else, somehow he would solve Autumn's business problem for her. He would come up with an idea to make her business profitable so she could pay whatever rent this new rancher would expect. He just had to.

"I've been praying about it," he said, "but I'll also put some thought into some viable ideas." Confidence exuded from his voice.

"That'd be great." But her defeated body posture spoke volumes.

Images flashed in his mind: the moment she discovered the pregnancy, the day the doctor did a sonogram and failed to find a heartbeat, the emotionally painful miscarriage.

No. His gaze sharpened on the darkening pasture in front of him. He hadn't been there for her when she needed him. Now he had the opportunity to fix this problem of hers. Years ago, she'd gone through a lot alone and suffered a great loss.

She was a hero in his eyes, and he wanted her to see him as her champion.

Chapter Ten

A week and a half later, Wyatt followed Autumn into a Triple C Ranch pasture to do some field training. Tallulah and Baby ran ahead of them as though they knew the destination.

Autumn turned and graced him with a charming smile. His heart skipped a beat at her attention. He returned her grin and his mind went back to the almost-kiss in the park. He really liked Autumn more than a friend, but having another relationship scared him. Anyway, he wasn't sure of her feelings for him.

"How's Harper been at day care?" Her hand brushed against his as they walked.

He let out a satisfied sigh. "I'm so proud of her. I've had a couple of calls lately, but since they let me speak with her, she has calmed down. Every day since our celebratory dinner has been a full day."

"Praise God." As she spoke, she touched his shoulder for a moment.

"Absolutely," he replied. These conversations, these sweet touches. He could get used to this easygoing friendship they'd built, but he was still wary of a romance. He lifted the plastic container of a dozen tennis balls he'd carefully been carrying so the balls didn't tip over and come in contact with the lid. "I rubbed one of the scented cotton balls on the inside lid of this container, so the tennis balls now carry Tanner's low blood sugar scent."

She opened the gate, and the dogs rushed through, then she closed it behind them. "Last time we played fetch like normal. You threw the ball and released Tallulah with the search command. When she returned the ball, you put that ball aside because it had fresh odors from bouncing on the ground."

"Yes." He was pleased she remembered everything in such detail. "We want the ball we are using to be as clean as possible. That way, it'll teach her the odor she is to search for."

"I've read the dog's ability to smell can be up to one hundred thousand times more acute than a human." He nodded, impressed with her knowledge. "So, are we going to play fetch again today, or what?" She stopped at the shaded tree stump they had used as a table last time.

He placed the container on the stump and pulled the ball launcher from his back pocket. "You'll see," he said, thrilled he had gotten to know Autumn again. He really liked her. A lot.

Autumn called Baby, picked her up and settled the dog in her arms.

He put a scented tennis ball in the launcher, called Tallulah over and placed her in a sit stay. "We're going to expand on what we did last time. Now adding what's called the scent cone by letting the ball settle before I release Tallulah to fetch." Knowing she'd be excited when the ball was thrown, he reached down and put two fingers under her collar and then launched the ball.

Tallulah watched the ball fly over the field and squirmed to go after it. He waited until the ball had stopped bouncing before saying *search* and then releasing Tallulah.

Autumn chuckled. "She was frustrated with you."

"Yes, that was the goal. To let her frustration build so she'd be even more excited about fetching."

Tallulah raced to the spot where she saw it last and then used her nose to find the ball. She clamped her jaw around the bright yellow treasure and started back.

Autumn's gorgeous eyes widened. "Wow, that was amazing. How'd she do that?"

"A scent cone is created when the ball lands on the ground and then bounces to a stop. After I told her to search and released her, she picked up the odor in the scent cone area until she found the ball."

Tallulah returned, and he placed the offered ball in the other container he'd brought so as not to introduce any other odors to the fresh scent balls.

"Can I do it?" she asked.

"Sure." He handed the launcher to her.

He held Tallulah back while Autumn threw a scent ball. Once it landed, he said *search* and released the dog. She went right to it.

"How come she didn't need to pick up the scent that time?"

Tallulah raced back and gave him the ball. "She saw where it landed, so she didn't need the scent cone. We have to throw it farther."

"Then you do it." She chuckled and handed him back the launcher. Baby was still snuggled in her arms, seemingly not interested in fetching herself.

He launched a fresh ball a few more times and Tallulah did great. The sixth time, she ran around for a bit before finding it.

"Why do you think one was harder?" she asked.

"Scent detection takes perseverance on the dog's part.

They need to continue to work to find the odor. Some dogs will give up," he said, taking the ball from Tallulah and scratching her behind the ears. "But she's doing a great job, aren't you, girl?"

He glanced at Autumn. Her grin was wider than he'd ever seen. She was absolutely gorgeous. "You did a great job selecting her as a service dog." A blush crept up her neck and slid to her cheeks. Her determination for the success of her business appealed to him.

"Thanks," she said. "What's next?"

Tallulah had lain down not far away, panting.

"I think we're done for today. Even though she could run forever, I'd like to end our training on a high note." He closed up the two ball containers. "Next time, we'll do the same thing, but after the ball stops moving, I'll spin her around and then release her. It sets up a little confusion and will force her to rely more on scent than eyesight." He gathered his supplies, and they headed back.

The smile blooming on Autumn's face was unstoppable, and he liked to think it was because of his dog training skills. Baby jumped down from her owner's arms to race after Tallulah.

Right then, he remembered the exciting idea he'd come up with last night to help her business succeed. He'd never dreamed that making Autumn happy would come to mean so much to him, and he didn't want to let her down. He had done that seven years ago and promised himself never again. She was such an upbeat person by nature. It had been hard to hear her defeated tone the other night, discussing the possible demise of her business.

She opened the gate, and they all went through before she secured it behind them.

"I have an idea to infuse cash into your business."

Autumn whipped around. "I'm all ears." The expectant look on her face made him feel all soft inside.

"I was thinking if you added dog grooming to your business, that might do the trick."

She cocked her head to the side, thought for a moment and then clapped her hands together. "I love that idea." She grinned at him like he'd hung the moon.

He was thankful he could help her. Especially after all she went through because of the pregnancy. He needed to make things right.

Also, he really enjoyed teaming up with her. He could see how she planned to help people, and once they got into the swing of things, they'd be able to help increasingly more clients. All because of Autumn's huge heart.

"So, how do I add that element to my business?"

"Water," he said. "I already checked the barn and there is no spigot."

"I know. I have to lug containers up the hill from my parents' house every day."

As her parents' house came into focus, he realized he had to come up with a solution so she could add grooming to her business. If the new owner allowed her to use the barn, he'd surely want some type of compensation. Wyatt had seen her books and right now, she had little to offer.

"I'm unsure you could run it from the Triple C. It'd probably need to be run from Henry's—"

"That won't happen. At least not while he's selling."

A flash of disappointment in her mesmerizing green eyes landed on him with the force of a physical blow, and something inside him surged.

If he had anything to say about it, her business would succeed. Seemed like the least he could do for her after he'd all but abandoned her seven years ago.

He pulled on her parents' garage door handle, slid it up and searched the walls, but found no utility sink and no exposed plumbing. "Bummer, no plumbing at all."

Autumn sighed. "Good thought, Wyatt. I appreciate you thinking out of the box for me." Though her words were kind, she appeared crushed that his brilliant idea would never come to fruition.

"Wait, if there's plumbing not too far away, you could hire a plumber for a minimal fee." He turned and wove back through the old furniture and boxes cluttering the space. "They have a laundry room, right?"

Autumn passed him. "Yes, right through this door." Excitement laced her tone.

They entered the house, and Autumn flipped on the overhead light.

He pointed at the washing machine. "Plumbing." He'd never felt so giddy about seeing appliances before.

She looked at the washer for a moment until understanding dawned. She clapped again, this time with even more glee. The excitement in her features warmed his core. He could get used to pleasing her.

"How much do you think it would cost?" She rushed into the garage, closing the laundry room door behind them, and inspected the drywall on the other side of the washing machine.

"I'm no plumber, but maybe a hundred or so to run the lines into the garage, then you'd have to purchase a utility sink or some type of dog bathtub." He shrugged. "It could cost a lot or not much, I'm not sure."

She was so excited that she threw her arms around him. He could smell her floral shampoo and breathed deeply, enjoying the moment. But then she jumped back. Probably realizing that hugging him was a bad idea.

He agreed. He'd gone through this giddy feeling with his ex-wife and allowed himself to get caught up in it. Back then, he hadn't had a four-year-old whose heart could get shattered as well.

"Sorry about that," she said. "I was just so excited." She lifted on her toes and put her dainty palm on his forearm. He resisted the urge to push an errant lock of hair away from her face.

"Thank you," she said. "Once Henry sells, this idea could be the reason my business succeeds."

He gazed into her eyes, then focused on her lips. Maybe he'd been mistaken when he was thankful for the interruption at the park. Maybe a romance with Autumn could work.

Autumn's phone played a tune. Still beaming, she took a step back and looked at the display. "Oh, this is about the festival. Let me take this." She answered and walked into the sunshine.

Wyatt's chest tightened, pride shooting through his core that he'd possibly come up with a solution to her business troubles.

His mind traveled to the past few evenings when they'd chatted until the wee hours of the night while sitting in old lawn chairs outside his apartment door.

If what they had wasn't a connection, he wasn't sure what it was.

Except, the last time he gave his heart to a woman, she trampled all over it and did worse to Harper. He'd have to tread cautiously to make sure that didn't happen again.

With her cell phone pressed to her ear, Autumn strode out of the garage and toward the shade of the dog barn. "Agnes, how are those new great-grandbabies of yours?

Twin boys, right?" The words were personal and kind, but inside Autumn's stomach turned over with whatever bad news she was about to hear. Because the festival steward never called with good news.

Agnes gushed about the babies. How they'd come six weeks early and had to stay in the NICU a whole week before going home. But now everyone was settled, and the babies were as fat as ticks.

Autumn chuckled at her Southern saying. "Congratulations, I'm so happy for you." She was sure she'd see the twins at the festival since Annie, their mother, was a friend of Autumn's.

Once in the dog barn, she settled on a hay bale and Baby jumped into her arms, as though the dog knew she needed emotional support. She stroked the soft fur under the terrier's chin for comfort. After sharing her past with Wyatt and then her mother, Baby's comfort wasn't as necessary as it had been. *Thank you, Lord, for helping me heal from my past and allowing me to have the strength to step into my future.*

She glanced down the hill and saw Wyatt pulling the garage door closed. Her tummy flipped at the memory of when he gazed into her face and focused on her lips. Had he thought about kissing her? She sure hoped so.

"Thank you, darlin'," Agnes responded. "Now I'm calling on official business." Agnes's tone turned serious. "Serenity Days Arts and Crafts Festival is only two weeks away. Can you believe it? Anyway, I was going through the booth requests and we do them in order of when they were submitted. Did you know that?"

Autumn grimaced. She'd been a little delayed getting her form in, but figured no one else would want to be on the exterior of the tent. Memorial Day weekend was usually hot and humid, and booths inside the tent were shady and had large industrial fans blowing. "I'll have dogs, so I thought it would make sense for my booth to be outside."

"Well, since the outside booths are cheaper, they fill up first. Yours will have to be on the inside, Autumn. Sorry about that."

Her stomach plummeted with the news. "It's okay. I'll pay the inside fee if you can put me outside."

"I can't do that."

"But, Agnes, I have dogs." She hated the pleading tone her voice had taken on, but she had no choice. "They bark, need to do their stuff, and you know, I think the other businesses and certainly the customers would be pleased to have us on the perimeter."

"Maybe, but I have my marching orders," Agnes said, a bit of irritation in her voice. "Tell you what, on the day you set up your booth, you can ask around and maybe someone will swap with you."

"Oh, good idea, Agnes. Thanks for the heads-up."

She slid her phone in her back pocket and sighed. "Not the news I was hoping for, Baby." She hoped she'd be able to find someone willing to switch booth locations with her.

"Taking a nap?" Wyatt asked, interrupting her musings as he entered the barn.

Her heart stuttered at the sight of the gorgeous man with a worn Stetson in hand.

The kenneled dogs began barking at the possibility of someone else who might feed them or let them play in a pen with their friends.

She smiled up at him. Somehow, she only needed to be in Wyatt's presence to feel calm. She was falling for him and couldn't seem to stop the momentum. The grooming idea had been brilliant. She needed to get herself in a position where she'd be able to pay some sort of rent to the new owner. Though Wyatt's idea might not make a ton of money, every bit would help.

Autumn put Baby on the ground and stood so she could hear over the barking. She told him about Agnes's call and how they were going to have to do some begging on setup day.

He touched her hand. "It'll work out. I can't imagine we won't be able to find someone who'd prefer to be in the shade with fans blowing on them."

Her skin tingled with the contact.

When his gaze flicked to her lips for the second time today, and he didn't lean in, Autumn knew he was afraid. His ex-wife had dragged him through the emotional wringer, along with Harper. She didn't blame Wyatt for his reticence to start up a relationship with her.

Except she'd never been so sure about anything.

It had taken her ten years to figure out a career that excited her, and the same amount of time to care deeply about a man.

Yes, she could back away and let this fear win. But that would be the easy way out.

She'd been dreaming of his lips on hers since that day in the park when he had almost kissed her, or so she thought.

She leaned in, but right then footsteps sounded on the gravel and they shot apart.

Autumn made like she was fixing her hair to keep whoever was standing there from seeing her flushed cheeks.

"Daddy, there you are."

Harper jumped into his arms and gave him an update on the soup she was making with Autumn's mother while Autumn's nerves trembled with almost getting caught in his arms.

Suddenly, she remembered he worked for her. They should probably keep things professional since she finally had the business of her dreams, and she didn't want to mess that up.

"Guess what?" Harper put her little hands on her father's cheeks to get his full attention.

"What, Sweet Pea?" His smirk was so incredibly adorable.

"Autumn's mother told me that I can go to her summer camp in just a couple of years." She squealed. "Can you believe it?"

Harper swiveled. "Is it fun, Miss Autumn? Is it?" Her eyes were sparkling and excited.

"Yes, Bug, it is. Everyone who attends has a great time."

Harper wriggled down from her father's arms. "What do the kids do, Miss Autumn? Coloring? Or math?" She scrunched up her nose.

"No math," Autumn said, then she told Harper all about summer camp. The petting zoo, pony rides, archery and how she would learn to take care of animals and grow her own vegetables.

"Yippee, I can't wait." She did an adorable, awkward dance. "Oh, and Mrs. McCaw told me to call her Memaw." The little girl's grin was huge, likely because her two best friends, Zoe and Tori, also got to call Autumn's mother Memaw.

For seven years, Autumn had believed she wasn't maternal. Wasn't capable of being a mother. But now she was wondering if that was a lie she had told herself. Maybe, just maybe, her dream of being a mother might someday come true.

Autumn smiled at the little girl who'd fostered this hope in her heart. "You don't say."

"I just said it," she giggled. "You're silly." Then she put her arms around Autumn and hugged her tight. "So it's almost like you're my mom." Harper bounced on her toes with her pronouncement.

Stunned, Autumn peeked at Wyatt. *I'm sorry*, he mouthed.

Her eyes grew watery at his apology as Harper rushed out to the grass chasing Buster. Wyatt didn't consider her worthy enough to mother his child. But before he could say a word, her phone dinged with an incoming text.

She rose and pulled her phone out to read the display, then glanced at Wyatt. "Henry." He moved closer so he could read the text over her shoulder.

Buyer is okay with you using the barn, but he wants rent money starting day one.

Excited she could keep using the barn but nervous about the potential price she might not be able to afford, she groaned, then asked if he knew how much.

Unsure. I'll ask him.

She lifted her gaze to Wyatt's. She saw strength and a bit of doubt on his handsome face.

Would they be able to turn a profit to pay the new owner's rent, or would she lose this business she loved?

Chapter Eleven

❧

"Play bubbles with me, Daddy?" Harper handed him the wand, the tray and the bottle.

"Go ahead," Autumn told him, a mixture of concern about the upcoming meeting and affection for Harper in her voice. "Our client should be here in about five minutes."

Wyatt nodded. It had been a few days since he'd come up with the dog grooming idea. He puffed his chest out, remembering Autumn's excitement, how she threw her arms around him and hugged tight, and how feminine she smelled up close. The plumber would be here tomorrow to give her a quote. Hopefully, it would be low enough that she'd be able to afford it.

Wyatt trailed after his daughter, not looking forward to the conversation he and Autumn had to have with their client. But Debra deserved to know Buster's status, and that they couldn't come close to meeting the deadline Autumn had promised her because they had to start over with a new dog.

He had even allowed Buster to roam free on the ranch when not being trained, so he'd come into contact with more distractions and maybe work out his attention span issue, but it hadn't helped. Buster's freedom had only allowed Harper to become the border collie's new best friend.

A month and a half in Serenity, working for Autumn,

and he was all in. With the business and maybe even with Autumn.

He placed the tray on the grass, poured a bit of the bubble solution into it and made giant bubbles for Harper to run through.

His daughter had come so far since they had arrived at this ranch. She no longer had meltdowns or tantrums at day care, and her night terrors were almost completely gone. Apparently, all she had needed was a new place, somewhere safe and homelike, far from her destructive mother.

"Hey there," Autumn said as she and Baby came over.

As soon as the terrier spotted Harper running around, she wriggled out of Autumn's arms. Harper squealed and raced in circles as Baby chased after her, a game Harper had discovered on her second day at the ranch.

He settled the wand in the puddle of liquid and faced Autumn. His pulse raced at her nearness. There was something about her that attracted him more than any other time in his life. The sun glinted off her wavy blond hair, but his gaze dropped to the curve of her full lips, the bottom one caught between her teeth in a moment of worry.

"It'll be okay. Debra will understand." Was she saying that for both their accounts?

Except their client was the last thing he was thinking of. The kiss they almost shared a few days ago was in the forefront of his mind. As well as the sweet discussions they had on his little landing about absolutely nothing after Harper went to bed each night. He treasured his time spent with Autumn.

She dragged her attention away from him and over his shoulder. "She's going to sleep well." Autumn chuckled.

"Agreed. She's been sleeping great ever since we moved to the ranch. Thank you for taking a chance on me, because this ranch and that apartment are doing wonders for Harper's well-being."

Never comfortable with praise, she bumped her shoulder against his upper arm in jest, and an easy silence settled between them. Only interrupted by Harper's squeals, Baby's yips and cows mooing in the distance. He wished he could bottle this moment with Autumn, because this was pretty close to perfection.

"How is Destiny going to take the news?" She teared up, speaking of the little girl desiring an allergy detection service dog. "She's visited Buster so many times and they've created a tight bond. After that close call in kindergarten, she was expecting to have him for the start of first grade."

Autumn had told him about the time someone in class had peanut butter crackers as a snack, even though Debra had told the administration all about her daughter's severe allergy. When Destiny broke out in hives and had difficulty breathing, the school had contacted an ambulance. The whole situation petrified both the teacher and the students. That day, Debra contacted someone who eventually put her in touch with Autumn to provide a scent-trained service dog to keep her precious daughter safe.

He wrapped Autumn up in a quick hug to comfort her, fully aware that Harper might see the affection.

"I'm sorry." Except, words wouldn't fix Buster. They wouldn't make the woman he cared about stop hurting.

The downside of caring for someone was that when they hurt, you hurt. Right now, his heart was breaking in two, seeing Autumn in anguish.

She leaned back and swiped a hand under her eye. "These animals have my heart from the moment they arrive here. What'll happen to Buster now?"

She blew out a breath and a strand of hair flew up and

settled on her cheek. He longed to tuck it behind her ear, but he hadn't earned the right to touch her like that. It didn't stop his fingers from itching for the physical contact.

"Where is Debra?" Autumn asked as she glanced at her watch. "She's late."

They settled on the grass to wait while they watched Harper enjoy the freedom only a ranch could give her. Her little girl giggles wound around his heart and squeezed. He wished he could bottle up the innocence of this stage of life.

Watching his daughter play on this sunny May day with Autumn by his side felt absolutely wonderful.

When Debra pulled into the gravel lot, Autumn stood and brushed her off her jeans. "Showtime." She glanced at her watch again and frowned. "An hour late. Unbelievable."

After Autumn introduced them to Wyatt, they went into the dog barn for some shade. Autumn had moved all the dogs into outside pens so they'd have some privacy.

"Daddy, look," Harper said as she jumped up and down, waving across the way at Laney and her twins in their back-yard. "Can I go play?" she asked, right as Laney motioned for his daughter to come over. Since Debra seemed a little high-strung before she even heard the bad news, he told Harper to head over. After Laney let his daughter into her backyard and waved at him, he turned his attention back to the client.

Wyatt had a bad feeling about this. Even though Debra lavished praise on Autumn and on snagging what she heard was the best dog trainer around, he saw moments of hard edges on her, as though she might be putting on an act and only pretending to be nice.

Autumn pulled two folding chairs for her client and daughter while she and Wyatt settled on hay bales. Thankfully, Autumn had gotten those chairs from her mother's camp. Debra seemed prim and proper and appeared uneasy in a barn, so sitting on a hay bale wouldn't cut it. And for such a young kid, Destiny seemed nervous.

He cleared his throat. "We wanted to discuss Buster's progress."

Destiny's face lit up. "I can't wait for my doggie to live with us. Mommy says he can sleep in my bed."

He glanced at Autumn, who nibbled on her lower lip.

"Part of being a service dog is behaving in public spaces," he said. "Unfortunately, Buster gets distracted in crowds."

Debra's frowned. "What are you saying?"

"Because Buster gets distracted in public spaces," he stated, "he will not work as a service dog."

"But she promised us." The mother glared at Autumn right as Destiny began wailing, tears streaming down her face. Debra's ruthless side had emerged.

Wyatt should have known. People pretend to be genuine but weren't. At the end of the day, everyone was just out for themselves.

Autumn looked like she was about to cry. He glanced between the two women and knew he had to fix this. For Autumn.

He had assumed Debra would be okay with this decision, because she'd want the best for her daughter. Yes, she'd be disappointed, but she'd understand.

Autumn's face was tight as she kept apologizing. His heart went out to her, because she worked so hard on her mission of connecting trained dogs with people in need.

No matter what happened with his relationship with Autumn, he wanted her business to succeed. She was wrapped up in the dog boarding and grooming so that she could provide these scent-trained service dogs.

He respected her vision and her.

He wanted her to succeed, and he certainly didn't want any retaliation from Debra.

"No. This is unacceptable," Debra stated. "Our daughter loves Buster. You have to make it work."

Autumn started to speak, but Wyatt touched her knee in an *I've got this* gesture. "A service dog that fails is referred to as washed out. But Destiny is more than welcome to adopt Buster," he said. "In fact, she could take him home today."

"Can I, Mommy?" Destiny's sad face brightened.

Hope stirred. Maybe everyone would win today. Destiny would get Buster, and Debra would accept they'd found another dog to train for her daughter's needs.

"Absolutely not." Debra scowled and stood, then pointed her finger at Wyatt. "If Autumn had hired a real dog trainer instead of some handsome cowboy, we wouldn't be having this conversation."

Before their client could turn to leave, Autumn jumped to her feet and pleaded with her to stay. They had a plan and she wanted Debra to hear it.

But all he heard was how unworthy and unfit Debra considered him. He leaned against the barn wall and realized she was right. Somehow, while he'd been playing at this new life in Serenity, he'd forgotten he was wholly unworthy of true love. His father had taught him that, and Chloe had reinforced the fact.

He glanced at Autumn, desperately trying to get her client to listen. She was so focused and passionate about her business, especially getting trained dogs into the hands of people in need.

He hadn't expected Debra to become so angry. Maybe he had messed up his explanation and set her off.

The last thing he wanted was to hurt Autumn's business. But it looked like he had done just that.

* * *

As her agitated client resettled herself on the chair, Autumn's chest pounded. She hadn't anticipated Debra would become so distressed by the news that Buster was a service fail. She knew she'd be unhappy, but this? She had wanted honest and open communication with all her clients. Maybe she should have taken the lead and broken the news to her client rather than Wyatt. Debra seemed to have faith in her. She didn't know Wyatt and distrusted outsiders. That sugary speech Debra gave about Autumn hiring Wyatt, the best dog trainer around, now seemed fake.

Destiny climbed into her mother's lap and shoved her first two fingers into her mouth. Debra unwrapped her clenched arms to secure her daughter, but her irritated expression remained in place.

Autumn settled on her hay bale next to Wyatt. Right now, she needed his encouragement and strength. She glanced at him and the worry and pain that swam on his face made her heart pinch. Baby placed her snout on Autumn's thigh. She lifted her furry companion into her lap.

She had been so concerned about losing Debra as a client that she'd all but ignored her snide comment, *if Autumn had hired a real dog trainer instead of some handsome cowboy, we wouldn't be having this conversation.*

Wyatt didn't think this situation was his fault, did he? She fumed over Debra's careless words. Her client's mistaken opinion gave Autumn the boldness she needed to rein in this conversation. No way was she going to allow someone to believe Wyatt was a subpar dog trainer. They should all feel honored he'd landed in Serenity and accepted her nonpaying job.

"Debra, I'm so sorry this has happened," she started.

"You better be," her client spat out. "You've broken my

daughter's heart." She tightened her arms around Destiny, and what seemed like a permanent frown deepened on Debra's face.

This wasn't working. Autumn needed to take a different tack. She peeked at Wyatt. She could do this. Seemed she felt stronger and wiser whenever he was around.

She cleared her throat, Wyatt's presence gave her clarity. "You said earlier how you heard Wyatt was the best dog trainer around."

"Clearly, the rumors were wrong." The disdain in her voice reverberated around the dog barn walls.

Autumn's business was at stake, and her reputation. Coupling people in need with an appropriate service dog required trust. If Debra started complaining about Autumn and her services, she wouldn't have to worry about making enough money for rent because she wouldn't have a business left to fight for.

Autumn put her hands up, as if to stop the barrage of insults on her client's tongue. "Debra, unfortunately, more service dogs are released from training programs for socialization than for any other reason." Beside her, Wyatt nodded in agreement as he shifted slightly closer to her. She appreciated his silent leadership. With him, she felt she had the courage to do anything.

"We're really sorry," Autumn firmly stated, "but it's best for Buster to be adopted as a loyal pet for someone. He cannot be a successful service dog, no matter how much training we give him."

Debra's expression remained pinched, but at least her verbal attack had ended.

Wyatt proceeded to gently tell her about the other dog they'd recently adopted and that he'd already tested her in public places and she had passed with flying colors.

"Would you like to meet her?" he asked, trying to entice the duo to forgive them for this unintentional change in plans.

His words were so gentle and encouraging. Maybe, just maybe, her client would give Autumn a reprieve.

"Absolutely not," Debra snipped. "I won't allow you to break my little girl's heart again. No, we'll wait until she's trained." The two rose from the chair, Debra firmly putting her hand on her daughter's shoulder, directing her to the car. Destiny kept looking over her shoulder with longing, as though she wanted to meet her new service dog, but her mother kept pushing her toward their luxury SUV.

Autumn was determined to have Wyatt work double time to get the new dog ready quickly. Destiny lived in fear during school snack time, and Autumn was steadfast in wanting to provide a scent-trained service dog to help the little girl face her fears even if her mother was mean. Baby spotted something in the distance, gave a bark and raced toward the pasture.

Autumn appreciated Wyatt's calm presence as the duo walked away. Right as Debra stepped into the sunlight, she turned around.

"I don't forget people who break promises," Debra hissed at Autumn, then turned and made her way down the hill to her vehicle.

Wyatt gathered her into a hug, and she sank into his embrace. She hadn't thought the conversation would go so badly. She swallowed the lump in her throat, savoring Wyatt's strength.

She pulled away from him, tears filling her eyes, making his handsome appearance wavy. "What if she interferes with us finding new boarding and service dog clients?" Tears threatened to stream down her face. It wouldn't take much for Debra to ruin her plan to make enough funds so she'd have some rent money for the use of the dog barn.

Wyatt rubbed her shoulders, soothing her runaway thoughts. "She won't sully your name. She's just surprised and upset right now. She'll come to her senses." His level-headed words helped her compose herself.

"You don't know her," Autumn said, then sniffed and wiped at her eyes.

Harper's sweet giggle brought her back to reality. Autumn set her jaw. Crying would not solve the problem. Somehow she'd have to fix this situation, but how? Destiny had already fallen for Buster. Maybe Autumn shouldn't have introduced the two until she'd gotten her trainer's okay.

But there was no such thing as a time machine. Anyway, if it weren't for Wyatt, she'd not be meeting the promised date for Tallulah. She also would not be receiving calls from potential clients and a well-known therapist with numerous patients in need.

She shot Wyatt a wan smile for trying to cheer her up and then scurried over to Buster's outdoor pen. She awkwardly settled the border collie in her arms and he swiped his scratchy tongue up the side of her face. The other dogs jumped at her legs, vying for attention. She couldn't help but care about each of these dogs, but what would happen to Buster now?

She set Buster down and he frolicked around with the other dogs, probably thrilled with the attention that no one else had been given. Did he know his life was changing? Wyatt came up behind her.

"Are you sure he won't work?" she asked with a whisper, already knowing the answer.

"Yes. We'd do Destiny a disservice if we continued to try."

She had poured countless hours into Buster so he'd be there for Destiny one day real soon. All for naught.

"It's not your fault." She appreciated how much he cared about her business. But what she liked most about him were the long talks each evening. Seemed they could talk about anything and nothing.

She focused on the frolicking dog. She adored Buster. He could stay at the Triple C, but her plan wasn't to collect dogs for herself, but to train dogs to make other people's lives better. Her eyes filled again and she pushed the emotion away. Telling Debra had been the right thing to do.

Baby raced over, and she picked up the terrier to snuggle. Wyatt corralled Tallulah and began training the pretty black dog with striking white marks.

Even though Wyatt was doing his own thing, she felt his gaze follow her. She could tell he cared about her and her feelings and this business of hers. She appreciated how he had stayed by her side while they talked with Debra.

Her phone buzzed in her pocket. She put Baby down and pulled her cell out. Henry.

She pressed her eyes closed and breathed a short prayer for good news before answering.

Henry confirmed the buyer would allow her to continue to use the barn for her business. Relief swooshed out of her. Then he named the monthly rent the buyer expected her to pay and her chest constricted.

An unattainable amount. There was no way she'd be able to meet that demand. Not even in a year or two.

Fifty bucks was about as doable as she could imagine, but the amount Henry quoted? No. She might as well close up shop today.

Chapter Twelve

Autumn clutched the box of flyers advertising the Serenity Days Arts and Crafts Festival that started on Saturday. She and Wyatt hoped to give the farmers market vendors small stacks to hand out. One side of the postcard-sized flyer advertised the festival, the other side advertised her business and highlighted their scent-based service dog training.

In the scorching sun, she and Wyatt trudged across the beaten down grass parking lot toward the farmers market pavilion in Love Valley, about twenty minutes from the Triple C. In her twenty-eight years, she'd never been here before. Yet somehow Wyatt knew about this place.

"How'd you hear about this market?" she asked Wyatt, who smelled altogether enticing today.

"Last Friday I had a client who recommended it. He runs the place, so maybe we'll see him today." He craned his neck as though looking for the man.

She focused on the tranquility of the farmers market and tried to stop her mind buzzing with things on her task list. She shifted the bulky box to her other hand and focused on the reason they were here—to drum up customers for her fledging business. She peeked at Wyatt. Whenever she was with him, she always seemed to have fun. He looked her way and caught her ogling him. She quickly glanced away.

"What are you thinking about?"

Apparently, he had seen her staring. She tucked her hair behind her ear, flustered for the moment. Autumn was thrilled he'd come into her life six weeks ago. Although it'd been hard to deal with the events surrounding her pregnancy, she felt freer now. Debra had been right when she stated Autumn couldn't have hired a better dog trainer. Wyatt was the best.

"I guess I'm running through my to-do list for tomorrow in my head." And trying to forget the pessimistic phone call from Henry. Tomorrow they would find out where their booth would be located for the festival and do some begging to change it before setting it up.

He stopped and looked her in the eye. "Autumn, we are ready for tomorrow. We've done everything possible to prepare." He gave her a dazzling smile that made her heart stutter. "Enjoy today, because you are going to get so many new boarding and grooming clients."

He could calm her with just a few words. How did he do that? She wasn't sure, but she appreciated him more with each passing day.

"Thanks for the dog grooming idea. The plumber came and installed the plumbing and stainless steel tub in the garage." She just hoped it wasn't a waste of money, since the dog barn rental was kind of up in the air.

"I saw it last night," he said, excitement lacing his voice. "I love the push-in stairs for larger dogs to walk up so you don't have to heft them in."

They continued on their way to the pavilion that held the goods for sale and walked through a thick crowd.

Now if only the festival was as successful as she hoped, so she could pay rent. The amount Henry told her the new owner wanted still stunned her.

"I hope the grooming side of things is as successful as we hope," she said, "because I have no idea how I'm going to pay that astronomical amount to the new owner of the dog barn. I haven't even earned that much in a month. Ever."

"Easy. Negotiate."

She stopped and stared at him as people flowed around them. "How? I have nothing."

"I disagree. Obviously, the new owner doesn't have plans for the dog barn. Be honest with him about how much you can afford to pay, and let him know the amount will grow as you build your company."

She turned his words over. If the new owner didn't plan to use the dog barn, then her rent money would be gravy. Maybe she had more of a negotiating position than she realized. Hope bloomed. It couldn't hurt to try.

As they stepped into the shade of the pavilion, her hand brushed his and she bit back a smile. He was good for her. It seemed like her emotional growth got stunted by her experience seven years ago. Ever since her confession to her mother two weeks ago, she had found peace. Not the temporary, shallow kind she'd experienced from time to time since the miscarriage, but a true peace, which could only have come from God. She felt changed. Like she'd been able to flip the page of her life to the next chapter. Finally.

She glanced at Wyatt. Now she felt like she was making up for lost time.

If her bottom line flourished, it'd be because Wyatt had either come up with ideas to grow her business or given her the encouragement to push herself.

Thank you, God, for this possible second chance you have given me and Wyatt. Also, for showing me that I don't have to carry my burdens alone.

Her mother's words played in her mind. *God doesn't see any past moral failures. You are clean in his eyes.*

She hadn't felt clean. She'd felt unworthy.

But faith wasn't about feelings.

And a few weeks with a clear conscience had done wonders for her inner self.

As they maneuvered through the noisy space, they stopped at each counter to ask the owner if they'd be willing to take a stack of flyers and hand one to each customer. Every one of them happily agreed.

After they finished one row, they moved to the next. Autumn stopped in her tracks. "There's Debra and Destiny," she whispered. In the distance, she eyed the woman and her child, who hadn't yet glimpsed them.

"Come on," Wyatt said. They were one vendor away from the next row, so he simply wove them over to the next, and away from her agitated client. Such a leader, another thing she adored about him.

"Goodness, I hope Debra keeps her thoughts to herself about losing Buster as Destiny's service dog," she said.

"I think she just needs time. I'm sure she won't hold it against you."

Autumn slid a stack of flyers onto the next agreeable vendor's counter, thanked him and turned.

"What if Debra tries to ruin me?" She drank in his features. If it weren't for him, she'd have raced back to her car as soon as she spotted Debra and beat a hasty retreat. "She knows so many people, she could, you know?"

He took her hand and squeezed. "She won't do that." The warmth of his touch soothed her and took her mind off of Debra.

"If she spreads bad news about me, I probably won't get many new service dog clients," she stated. Her entire goal had been to place trained dogs with people in need of a specialized service dog, but they were only working on three right now. Her goal of many seemed far away.

Wyatt chuckled and pulled her to a stop. "Autumn, come on. With that therapist recommending you, we'll likely have to turn clients away. Even with you working on basic obedience and social skills with the rescue dogs to prepare them for the more deep dive training I'll give them, we only have so much time to devote to them. We want to make sure the service dogs are absolutely ready to be placed when we send them home."

She smiled up at him. "So true."

They continued on, his larger hand cradling hers. She found the show of affection comforting.

His compassion had drawn her in seven years ago, but she hadn't been ready for a relationship back then. She'd been so lost and confused. Now that she had a drive and focus, she was open to seeing where this led.

He guided her around a group of individuals chatting.

And who knew? Maybe her mother was right, maybe she had to go through the pregnancy and miscarriage seven years ago and everything else she'd endured, good and bad, to make her into the person she was today. An individual who had finally put the past behind her and was ready to give away her heart. If not for her past trials, she wouldn't be who she was today. She'd still be that selfish and lost person she hadn't liked too much herself.

A deep baritone voice called Wyatt's name.

They turned, hands still clasped, and a rotund man smiled at them. "When I told you about this place the other day, I didn't think you'd come, but I'm glad you made it," he said, then opened his hand as if presenting the space to them. "What do you think?"

Wyatt gave her a quick glance, let go of her hand and looked around. "It's great, Chester. Thanks for mentioning it to me."

"And who's this? I didn't know you had a girlfriend."

"Oh, she's not... I mean, this is Autumn." He scratched at his pinking neck like he was embarrassed. "I train service dogs for her."

She jerked her head back at his sterile description of their relationship. She thought they meant something to each other.

After shaking Autumn's hand, Chester turned to Wyatt, and they had a brief discussion about his pregnant dog.

Once Chester left, they both stood and watched him. The meeting had been awkward.

Wyatt took her hand and tugged her after him, as though the clumsiness of meeting Chester had never happened.

She followed Wyatt, but after his interaction with Chester, she was confused. Was he embarrassed to be seen with her?

She pulled her hand away and pretended to organize the remaining flyers in her grasp. Had she misunderstood his intentions?

Wyatt spoke to the next vendor and took some flyers out of her shrinking stack. She waved her thanks as they moved on.

This was the first time he had held her hand for an extended period. Maybe it was because they weren't at the Triple C or in Serenity near friends and family who could draw conclusions from the behavior.

Did this relationship only mean something to her? Or did Wyatt have a vested interest as well?

She hoped so, because she really liked him and could see a future with him and Harper.

* * *

Wyatt thanked the vendor and moved on. Today had confirmed his suspicion—he liked Autumn as much more than a friend. Since they'd reconnected a month and a half ago, he had fallen for her passion, her intelligence, her compassion and her fierce independence.

"Wanna peach?" A sharp knife with a hunk of dripping peach skewered on it shot in front of his face.

Surprised, Wyatt reared back against the older man's offering, while Autumn giggled at his side.

They shared a look at Wyatt pulled the slice of peach from the knife and the juices ran down his thumb. The sweet flavor exploded in his mouth. "Mmm," he said as he shut his eyes to enjoy the tangy, yet sweet flavor. "This is so good."

Autumn tried a piece from the aggressive peach peddler and agreed. They purchased a bag to split.

As they walked away, Autumn grabbed a piece of the fruit and stuck it in front of Wyatt's face. "Want a peach?"

They shared a belly laugh.

It felt good to be with her today. Real good. He rarely got time off these days. Though, working with the dogs was extremely satisfying, and being with Autumn was a joy. Maybe he had more fun in his current life than he realized.

But why had he clammed up when he saw Chester? He probably gave the man and Autumn the impression that he was ashamed of their blooming connection, but he wasn't.

He rubbed a hand over his face. He'd done it again. Seemed relationships just weren't his thing. But he really wanted to explore where this one led with Autumn. The crowd thickened, so he placed his hand on the small of her back to let her lead the way. She stopped to let a group pass, and he took that moment to apologize.

"I'm sorry about the mix up with Chester," he said.

She turned to him with a bland expression, as though he hadn't hurt her, but he knew he had. "No problem."

"My weird reaction to his question probably made you think I was embarrassed by you." She hugged herself, and he could tell the interaction had wounded her. "I'm the opposite of embarrassed. Most days, I wonder what you see in me."

A passerby bumped Autumn into him and she jumped back, but not before he saw a tender expression on her face.

"I think I'd like to explore where things between us lead, Autumn. What do you think?"

She gave him a small smile that grew as though she couldn't help herself. "I'd like that very much."

He touched her hand and her fingers curled around his like a hug.

"Let's finish," she said and lifted the small stack of flyers.

He waved at a vendor who already had their flyers. This place really was quaint. He hoped they'd get some solid business from handing out their advertisements.

"Do you see Debra anywhere?" She looked around.

He followed her gaze. "Maybe they left. Why are you so worried about her, anyway? It's not like one person has any say in your business."

Autumn halted. "Wyatt, you've got to be kidding me. Debra is on the town council. She can make or break my business."

Oh no! He hadn't known she had so much pull with the locals. "I'm sure she's just upset about Destiny's loss. She'll keep her mouth shut," he said, hoping that was true. He touched her fingertips to continue on their way, but before long, Autumn stopped to look at some earrings.

He checked emails on his phone while she shopped. She

bought a pair and gave a stack of flyers to the vendor, then she waved him over to the ice cream counter, seemingly having forgotten about Debra. The line wasn't too long, so he joined her and looked up at the handwritten board hanging above them to review the flavors.

"Black raspberry sounds good," he said.

She bumped his shoulder. "Are you kidding me? With triple chocolate and chocolate caramel cookie dough, you pick a berry choice? Ooh, wait, chocolate brownie extreme. That's the one."

He grinned. "So I take it you like chocolate ice cream?"

"Anything chocolate. Well, milk chocolate. I'm not a fan of dark chocolate." She chuckled as they moved up in line.

"So, I've been thinking about your Saturday obedience class idea."

She turned, and he gazed into her rosy face. Her wavy hair was pulled back in a messy bun, highlighting her cheekbones. His breath caught at the base of his throat at how gorgeous she was, inside and out.

"What if we offered an eight-week class and you shadow me, then you can take a meaningful role in the following session? Eventually you can teach it by yourself."

She nibbled on her kissable lower lip.

He took her fingers and gave them a light squeeze. "You can do it." He had such faith in her.

"Really? I'm not sure."

"Come on, Autumn, you've been training the service dogs on basic obedience as well as social skills. Frankly, you could teach the second session by yourself."

She clasped her fingers with his and leaned against his shoulder, releasing a satisfied sigh that wound around his heart. "You always make me believe in myself. Thank you."

He wished his arm was free so he could hug her and tell

her how amazing she was. How she could do anything she set her mind to.

But instead, they stepped forward and placed their ice cream orders, and he paid.

Even though they had both been extraordinarily busy since they met, they'd developed a deep friendship. One that he treasured.

His phone rang. He pulled it out to see the display of the day care. His stomach dropped. Obviously, Harper wasn't having a good day. He held his finger up in a *just a moment* motion, then answered.

He listened to the day care director and then asked to speak with Harper, hoping to resolve the issue without picking her up. When his daughter got on the phone, he could hear her whimpering and sniffling. He asked her what was wrong, and they talked through her concerns. Mostly, she was worried because she knew he was out of town today.

Autumn put her hand on his shoulder with a look of concern in her brilliant green eyes. She must have realized Harper was having a bad day.

"I'll pick you up before the other kids go home today and the three of us can go to the diner. How about that?" He winked at Autumn.

The way Autumn's eyes lit up made his heart pound extra fast.

"Can we do backward dinner?" Harper asked with excitement in her voice.

"Sure," he answered, eyeing his dripping cone. Once in a while, he allowed them to have dessert first.

His declaration of picking her up early, along with dessert before dinner, appeared to make her happy as Harper told him she couldn't wait and handed the phone back to the day care director.

"She okay?" Worry threaded through Autumn's face after he pocketed his phone.

"Yes. She was just concerned, since she knew I had left town this afternoon."

"Oh good." Autumn gazed around the space. "As soon as we're done with our cones, we can leave so we can pick her up, okay?"

He smiled as they settled into a little seating area to eat. That was one of the many things he liked about Autumn. She cared for Harper and her well-being.

While they ate, they chatted about the basic obedience class and how it would work. He could see her excitement as they talked.

They threw away their napkins and headed to his truck. Once seated, they both reached back to place their purchases in the back seat and their heads lightly bumped.

He apologized and chuckled, but as he looked into her eyes, mere inches from his, her plump lips caught his attention. He could hardly breathe as chemistry sizzled between them.

The moment stood still. Her sweet perfume enveloped him. A wayward strand of her hair tickled his cheek. He'd been contemplating the several kisses they'd almost shared.

Should he kiss her?

He inched closer to her face and her lips parted. He pressed a soft kiss against her full lips and felt the passion all the way down to his toes. He deepened the kiss, not wanting the moment between them to end.

She brought out the best in him. Gave him hope for the future. This was a woman he could fall hard for. Someone who wouldn't break his trust.

When he finally pulled back, he settled into the driver's seat. His lips still tingled.

Wow. He gave her a quick glance as she straightened her hair and seemed to be tongue-tied as well.

Attraction hummed between them, but it wasn't just their newfound chemistry. Ever since she'd told him about the past and had forgiven him, their time together had been natural. He respected her dedication to her family, her business sense and her passion to train dogs for people in need.

But did he have it in him to give another relationship a shot? After his marriage had failed, he didn't think he ever would, but Autumn was making him see things in a different light.

His father and Chloe had done their best to break his confidence in them. Could he learn to trust again?

Chapter Thirteen

❧

Wyatt grinned at the happy bantering among townspeople as they set up their booths the following day. Autumn had told him this was an arts and crafts festival, but Serenity Days Arts and Crafts Festival was impressive. Booths displayed food from local merchants, jewelry and note cards designed and made by teens and so much more.

Banners graced the old-timey downtown light posts advertising the festival. Many local merchants had used a removable spray paint to decorate their display windows and multicolor pennant flags graced the entrance to the enormous tent.

But before he and Autumn could prepare for tomorrow's hoped-for rush of customers, they'd need to swap booths with someone, as they required the overflow space the outdoor areas provided to have on-demand demos for customers.

Autumn had taken the other side of the narrow row of booths on the outside of the huge tent and in the direct sun. Their booth was in the shade, under the tent, and had an industrial fan a few feet away blowing on them. It'd be perfect for anyone who didn't have canines and didn't plan to hold impromptu dog training demos.

Wyatt's frustration grew when the last person on his side, a woman planning to do face painting, gave him an emphatic no. He thanked the lady and prayed that Autumn had met with success.

How come no one was willing to swap booths with them? He hadn't imagined this would be hard. If he and Autumn didn't require the extra outdoor space, he'd prefer to be under the tent with an industrial fan blowing on them, keeping them cool in this Memorial Day weekend heat. He rubbed the back of his now sweaty neck.

Autumn rushed up to him, Buster's leash in her hand, and grabbed his arm. Man, she was stunning, even in this hot and humid weather. "I ran into my friend Lily, who owns a party store and is promoting her new side business, custom decorated sugar cookies for special events." Her eyes sparkled with the enormous grin on her gorgeous face. "She totally forgot about the heat and sun when she signed up for her outside booth to save money and she's happy to swap with us. Grateful even."

Before he could think, he pulled her into a celebratory hug. She smelled all feminine and floral, a scent he'd come to adore. Their kiss from the other day lingered in his mind. Such a sweet and romantic moment. He hoped to have more of those. But before too many people saw their affection for one another, he let her go.

Her cheeks heated as though she was embarrassed. He got it, he really did. When his marriage fell apart, all their friends took sides. So he understood that hugging in public made a statement she might not be comfortable with. Yet.

While they set up the booth, Autumn tied Buster's leash to the folding table they'd gotten from the truck bed.

Every couple of minutes, someone stopped to ask about the border collie who'd been a service-fail for Destiny and Debra. They'd crouch, snuggle with him and ask if he was one of the service dogs in training. Autumn would tell them he wasn't. Buster was up for adoption. A couple of people stood and told her they'd think about it and get back to her after the weekend.

Each time, Autumn grabbed his upper arm and squeezed, a sparkle in her forest green eyes. "Maybe they'll be his new family. They sure seem nice, don't they?"

He appreciated how she brought him into the fold. Every day. Early on, she'd made him feel like a part of her business. Well, after they cleared the air about the pregnancy he'd known nothing about, which he still felt bad about. He continued to be amazed by how strong a woman Autumn had become.

Cora and his daughter headed into the booth. "Buster," Harper squealed as she let go of the older woman's hand and knelt in front of the dog, allowing him to cover her face with doggy kisses.

Wyatt and Autumn shared a meaningful glance at his daughter's obvious love for their failed service dog.

Each time someone expressed interest in Buster, it twisted Wyatt's insides because he knew how much Harper loved the dog. Not only did his daughter want a dog, but she needed one. Except, he wasn't sure what the future held and if he'd always be able to live in a place that accepted pets.

Cora checked to see if they needed help. Once she discovered they were almost set up, she moved on.

Harper caught sight of Trisha and Walker setting up their Harmony Equestrian Center booth with their three adopted children nearby. She rose. "Can I go play with Gabby?" she asked, almost all in one word.

Wyatt agreed and she skipped over to the family.

"You should adopt Buster. For Harper," Autumn whispered, almost as if she could read his mind.

He turned to her. "I'm seriously thinking that."

"I'd love it if Buster would go to a great family, because I feel horrible about adopting him and not recognizing he wouldn't succeed in social settings as a service dog."

"Don't keep beating yourself up. If I don't adopt him, someone else will. He's gotten a lot of positive comments today."

She frowned and nodded at the same time. He wanted to take her in his arms and comfort her. Tell her that Buster would end up with a good home. Maybe God had even been watching over Harper when Autumn had adopted Buster, because his daughter had connected with the dog from the start, much more than any other dog in Autumn's pack.

Autumn looked toward Harper, who was running around the Serenity Stables booth with four-year-old Gabby. Maybe he should tell her to slow down or have her come back to their space so as not to disrupt Walker and Trisha. Right then, the couple looked over and simply smiled at them, so Wyatt wasn't about to stop his daughter's fun.

Man, he was thankful for their move to Serenity and how the community had embraced them. He glanced at Autumn and his second chance at love.

"You don't think she'll fall, do you?" Autumn's brows scrunched together in concern.

He loved how she worried about Harper's safety. It proved to him how much she cared for his daughter. But did Autumn care for him like he cared for her?

"She's just fine. Walker and Trisha have their eye on her."

As they finished setting up the folding tables, his mind again wandered to their kiss yesterday. Though he had enjoyed it, traveling down this road scared him.

After their fun backward dinner last night, where Autumn played along and got apple pie à la mode to start, and then their time chatting after Harper turned in, he was drawn to Autumn even more. Though they had danced around the kiss and hadn't yet spoken of their feelings.

Autumn pulled out a festive tablecloth that they spread and then blue taped to the small folding table. She handed him a lengthy piece of tape while he got under the table to secure the tablecloth in place.

"Early this morning, I got a call from a psychiatrist in Love Valley. Apparently, she picked up a flyer we dropped off at the farmers market yesterday and wanted to know what our lead time on a service dog for anxiety was." She pumped her eyebrows with her excitement. "She has several clients and other organizations are at least a year out."

He was so happy for Autumn and her new business. It seemed to be taking off, and the main reason she'd started the business was to match people in need with service dogs.

"Turns out I'm not working a full forty hours even though I'm paid full time. Doc Earl seems to only book about six hours a day, and lots of Fridays are half days." He savored the enthusiasm covering her face. She was adorable when she leaned in and focused only on him. "So I'm feeling more confident with my availability to train service dogs. With you working on their socialization, it's speeding up the deadlines even more."

Her cheeks warmed at the compliment. When she gazed at the ground in embarrassment, he noticed an eyelash had fallen to her cheek. He reached over and gently flicked the lash away. Their gazes connected and desire warmed in his chest. He leaned closer.

"Daddy." Harper rushed over, out of breath and stepped between them, forcing them apart. She reached for his sweating water bottle and took a swig. "For a four-year-old,

Gabby's pretty fun," she stated, her cheeks red from the running and playing.

He and Autumn shared a look, and she broke out laughing.

"You're four too, Sweet Pea," he reminded her.

"I know. But since I go to day care, I'm much more mature than my peers." She riffled through the half-page flyers that Autumn had designed and printed.

Autumn's eyes twinkled at his daughter's silly comment. Though, he had always thought she was so mature because of the divorce and dealing with her mother, not because of day care.

"Have you ever played the ring toss game?" Autumn asked his daughter.

Harper flicked a glance at him and he shook his head. "No, why?" she asked.

Autumn told her all about the game and that it'd been her favorite when she'd been a young kid. Since it was one of the festival games, they decided they'd play it together tomorrow.

"Just you and me?" His daughter kept her gaze on the ground, apparently feeling a little insecure today.

Autumn squatted and took Harper's hands. "Yup. Pinky promise." They hooked their pinky fingers together and grinned.

"I wish you were my mommy." Harper's voice held a shy tone.

Autumn gave his daughter a big hug, then stood.

He sucked in a breath at Harper's heartfelt words while his heart hitched at her sweet innocence. He was her father and responsible for her in every way.

Was he doing the right thing by moving forward in this relationship with Autumn? It felt good at the moment, but Harper's heart was on the line.

"Oh, I almost forgot. I have T-shirts," Autumn stated, then winked at him.

She pulled a navy shirt out of her bag and handed it to him. The back read Triple C Ranch Dog Boarding and Training. On the front was Wyatt, Trainer.

He lowered his shirt to thank her, but she was handing Harper a much smaller one. The front of hers read Harper, Head Cheerleader.

His eyes misted that Autumn thought of including his daughter.

"I love it," Harper said.

"You are the best cheerleader around, Bug," Autumn said as she settled her bag on the folding chair.

He gave Autumn a quick hug and thanked her. He was overthinking things. No one's heart was going to get broken.

Any woman who treated his daughter like a princess was worth taking a chance on.

The look on Wyatt's face when he spotted Harper's T-shirt surprised Autumn. Why wouldn't she include the sweetest little girl she'd ever grown to love? It was as though he didn't want Autumn and Harper to have a relationship.

Was he jealous? Or maybe afraid she'd one day hurt his little girl like his ex-wife had?

Maybe he had a point, because she had become vulnerable to both Wyatt and Harper, and vulnerability led to betrayal. Maybe she should pull away from whatever was happening with the handsome dog trainer. The *yes, he's amazing* clashed deep inside with the *no, you could get hurt* and it made her feel dizzy.

Harper hugged her shirt. "Can I put it on? Can I?"

Autumn threw back her head and laughed. "Of course

you can." She helped her pull the tee over her clothing. Though she'd purchased an adult extra small, it still hung down to the little girl's knees. Harper insisted on having the dog graphic on the front because it was "so cute," so the Harper, Head Cheerleader logo was on her back.

Wyatt pressed his lips together to keep from laughing, and he had a point. She looked awfully charming.

"Looks adorable," she told Harper. She took a step back from Wyatt, who yesterday had kissed her senseless. Last night they had talked on his tiny porch for half the night about nothing, leaving a smile on her face that hadn't gone away since. That made his surprise that she'd included Harper in the T-shirts confusing.

When they'd reconnected a month and a half ago, she had decided they had too much history to develop a genuine connection. They'd already had their chance, and both had independently passed it by.

So why had her heart jumped past her head so quickly?

Maybe she should have kept their relationship all business? Except, somehow, it felt too late to turn things around now.

"Hey, sweetheart," her mom said as she approached and gave her a squeeze. "How's everything going?"

Excited for the festival and all the business she was hoping to drum up, she updated her mother on their progress and, since Buster was hot and panting from the heat, sent him home with her. Harper gave him a long hug before her mother trotted off with the dog.

"We're going to visit Tori and Zoe. We'll be back," Wyatt said, then turned toward the inner booths and blessed shade with Harper.

Autumn was grateful for her family's help with her business and forgiving attitude about her plight seven years ago.

She pulled out the flyers and business cards with her and Wyatt's cell phone numbers listed and stacked them on the small folding table. They were trying to keep as much floor space as possible for potential client discussions. She then stepped back and surveyed their little space with a critical eye. They were ready for tomorrow.

"Are you Autumn?"

"I am," she responded to the twenty-something pretty woman in front of her. Autumn wasn't sure if she was another booth holder or just someone from the town milling about. In Serenity, they didn't close off the area during setup. In fact, her mother had mentioned that Lily had already sold a bunch of decorated sugar cookies she'd brought with her.

"Hi," the woman said and extended her hand for a formal shake. "I'm Morgan and my brother Tyler is buying Henry Wright's property."

"Wow, it's so nice to meet you, Morgan." The new owner's sister looked superfriendly. Could she persuade Morgan to talk with her brother about the high rent? Because if she was unable to negotiate the sum down a lot, she couldn't afford to keep renting the space.

"So you train service dogs?" Morgan's eyes sparkled at the topic.

She told her new friend all about the process and that Wyatt was certified and had been training dogs for years.

"So what's your lead time in providing a service dog to a new client?"

Autumn faltered. Buster's inability to concentrate, which led to him being washed out, came to mind.

"I'm sorry," Morgan said. "I'm not nosing around, but my sister has a son with severe asthma, and I've read that a service dog could help him. He's such an active little boy and has no fear, not even the serious asthma."

Autumn nodded. "You're right. They train service dogs for asthma to remind a client to check his oxygen level, shortness of breath or medication levels."

"That sounds like what I read. Let me tell my sister about your business and I'll get back to you." Morgan reached in for a quick hug and then they exchanged contact information. She left, melting into the groupings of people preparing for tomorrow's big event.

If Autumn helped Morgan's sister, then maybe the woman could convince her brother to work with Autumn on the rent price.

Wyatt returned, Harper's little hand in his.

"What did the girls think of your shirt?"

Harper excitedly shared how Tori and Zoe wanted one of their own.

Autumn took in the pair, who'd begun to mean so much to her. "Thanks for all your help today." Her life was so full. Now all she needed was Tyler to relent on how much he required for rent.

"I thought you'd given up on this failure of a hobby." Debra stepped into view, her tone laced with contempt.

Autumn froze at the vindictive woman and her comment. She'd hoped Debra would go home and think about what had transpired with Buster and realize that his failure as their service dog was no one's fault. But apparently not.

An older lady stepped forward, wrapped her hand around Debra's elbow, then whispered something to her. Debra lifted her chin, glared at Autumn, turned around and stomped away. The older lady mouthed, *I'm sorry*, over her shoulder.

All the blood drained from Autumn's head as worry

clawed at her gut. Would Debra somehow sabotage the festival for her and Wyatt? Or worse yet, would she undermine Autumn's business so she'd be unable to pay the new dog barn owner the exorbitant rent he was requiring?

Wyatt wrapped his arm around her shoulder, and she sank into his embrace. "It'll be okay. She's just hurt for Destiny." He squeezed her fingers and her skin warmed with his touch. Oh, she was falling for this man. "Give them time. They'll get over it."

She tipped her head against his shoulder, relishing his confidence and thankful he'd come into her life.

He pressed a kiss against the top of her head, and butterflies took off in her stomach. Was this the real deal? Did they have a relationship that would stand the test of time? She hoped so, because not only did she like Wyatt a lot, but he had turned into one of her best friends as well.

"Can we get ice cream, please?" Harper implored as she tugged on Wyatt's arm.

He looked at Autumn. "We're done here, right?" At her shaky nod, he grinned. "Then I think the owner, trainer and head cheerleader deserve a break." The way he looked at Autumn made her feel like the three of them were the team she had been hoping they'd become.

Confidently, Harper turned toward What's the Scoop, the little ice-cream store in town, and held out a hand for each of them. That had been happening a lot lately, and Autumn had come to love it.

They strode down the busy sidewalk linked by hands. Almost like a real family.

The moment felt almost too good to be true. Here she was, being treated as though she belonged with them, and she longed to.

When she looked over at Wyatt, he beamed down at her,

and she realized she had everything she wanted right here. In this little hodgepodge family of three.

Her unease over Wyatt's reaction to Harper's declaration of motherhood for Autumn was clearly unfounded. With each step they took toward What's the Scoop, she allowed her doubts to drift away and settled into the rhythm of the life she'd never dreamed she could have.

"Triple C Ranch Dog Boarding and Training," a man said as he smiled down at her. He must have noticed their walking advertisement on Harper's backward T-shirt.

"I'm Tyler, the guy buying Henry Wright's property." They shook hands as Harper hid behind Wyatt's legs.

"I met your sister, Morgan, a little while ago."

"Really? That's nice. I'm kind of stoked to have some rent money coming in on day one. I think this situation will be a win-win for both of us."

Wyatt touched her arm, likely to indicate for her to let him take the lead, as he'd already come up with a negotiation plan.

"Welcome to Serenity," Wyatt said. "Since you're new here, you might not be aware that we just started this business. As all new ventures go, it takes a while before they actually become profitable, so Henry was allowing Autumn to use the dog barn at no cost."

Tyler's brows lifted. "Well, that just doesn't seem right." His surprised gaze bounced between trainer and owner, finally landing on Autumn. "I'm kind of set on the price Henry gave you. If you can't afford it, I have some plans myself for the barn." Before she could say another word, Tyler strode away and her stomach sank.

He had every right to use the barn, it was on his property after all.

Wyatt placed a protective arm around Autumn. "It'll all work out. We'll find somewhere new, I just know it."

But the look on his face didn't match the confidence in his voice.

They had been so sure they'd be able to negotiate with the new owner that Tyler's quick dismissal shocked her.

Autumn could barely breathe. It felt like a one-hundred-pound weight was sitting on her chest, and she couldn't wiggle away from the pressure. What if she and Tyler couldn't come to terms and she lost the dog barn?

Chapter Fourteen

The day of the festival had finally arrived. The town square hummed with activity and the air held the sweet smell of funnel cakes. Not only did residents attend, but people from nearby towns came to this festival as well.

Autumn had considered leaving Baby at home, but she was so well socialized that she was a walking testimony to the training business. Anyway, the terrier was adorable, which made many people stop to pet her. That gave Autumn an opening to talk with them about her business services. She pushed away the urgent need to find a new location because of Tyler's sky-high rent demand. She'd deal with that situation after the festival ended.

Edith, from the Confectionery Bakery, stopped by Autumn's booth with sweet-smelling samplings of doughnuts, frosted brownies, chocolate chip cookies and blueberry muffins. Harper took one of each, thanking Edith. The little paper cups held less than a bite, but the girl enjoyed each morsel.

Autumn snagged two brownie samples and asked Edith how her day was going as she downed the delectable treats. After seeing Debra yesterday, she could use some chocolate. She hoped the woman was nowhere to be found today.

"We're having great sales. Thanks for asking," Edith

replied. "Your daughter has wonderful manners." Before Autumn could correct her, she slipped away.

Many people grinned when they spotted Harper, and their sentiment filled Autumn with joy. She was the sweetest little girl ever. Now Autumn knew the pride her married brothers felt toward their children.

She laid a hand on Harper's shoulder. Wyatt had been called away to help Doc Earl with something. In the meantime, it was just the girls in the booth.

"Aw, is she friendly?" A lady stopped in front of them, eyes on Baby. After Autumn assured her the terrier was, the lady crouched down and scratched Baby's ears. "She is so adorable."

The lady then asked if Autumn offered basic obedience classes. Autumn told her about the plan, handed her a business card, and they parted ways.

"Miss Autumn, when are we going to the ring toss?" Harper asked.

"Soon, Bug, soon." She gave the girl a side hug and relished the moment.

She never imagined there would be a day where she was comfortable being in a mom role. But here she was. Who knew, if she and Wyatt continued down this path, perhaps one day she would be Harper's bonus mom. Her stomach flipped at the thought, both excited and nervous at the same time. Children were a blessing, but also an enormous responsibility.

She thanked God for bringing Wyatt back into her life and for healing her from the wounds surrounding her pregnancy and miscarriage that had led her to believe she wasn't meant to be a mother.

God had worked those painful things to grow her and mold her and prepare her for this surprising relationship.

"Autumn." Mabel from the Morning Grind coffee shop stopped at the booth. "We saw Wyatt's training demonstration earlier and are so excited about your new business. How many service dogs have you placed so far?" Expectation lined her wrinkled features.

"We are training three. One should be placed in July so the boy can feel confident going to camp and then starting kindergarten with diabetes." Harper tugged on Autumn's shorts.

"Can we go to the ring toss now? Please." Harper drew out the last word as though she would die if they didn't leave right at this moment.

Autumn shared a chuckle with the older lady. She crouched low to make eye contact with the girl. "In a minute, okay?" She stood and continued her spiel with Mabel. "And I have two more dogs we are training for clients, one for diabetic alert and the other as an allergy detection dog for a nut allergy." Assuming Debra calmed down and still wanted to work with them.

Mabel nodded, a look of delight on her face. "The town is so proud of you for starting a small business. We just know you'll be a success." Autumn thanked the woman for her support, but didn't mention she might lose her rental space. And without the dog barn her business might come to an end.

Behind Mabel, Autumn spotted Tyler and her eyes widened. Maybe now was the perfect time to talk him into letting her use the dog barn.

As Mabel turned, Autumn caught the man's attention, and he stepped to her table. *Lord, please touch Tyler's heart and allow him to understand my predicament so he'll be willing to negotiate with me.*

Harper tugged on Autumn's shorts, so she took a small step away. She needed to focus on this conversation.

She pasted on a smile and asked if he was enjoying himself.

"I am," he said. "This town is turning out to be everything I had hoped for."

"I'm so happy for you," she replied, then swiped at the nervous sweat building on her forehead. "I've been contemplating what you said yesterday, Tyler, and I was thinking that the barn is so far away from your other structures. It would make sense to let me use it, don't you think?"

"Can we go to the ring toss now?" Harper interrupted. She'd climbed onto the folding chair and was at eye level with them. Tyler laughed at her antics.

Autumn glanced at the girl and nodded. As soon as Wyatt returned to watch over the booth, they'd go play the game. But before she could get a word out, Tyler spoke.

"With a UTV, I can get to any of my outbuildings in a few minutes. So, no, it makes no sense to let you use the barn for free." He appeared as though her using the dog barn wasn't on his list of concerns.

She focused on the man and licked her lips. She had to convince Tyler to agree to a lower rent. How could Autumn get him to relent?

"How about I pay a smaller amount for now," she said, "and work my way up as my business grows?" That seemed like a reasonable request. She almost held her breath, hoping he'd agree.

He shook his head with what looked like regret. "The rent fee is non-negotiable." And just like yesterday, he turned and walked away before she could speak.

She wanted to rush after him, but what good would it do? He desired more rent money than she could afford. And apparently he had a plan to use the dog barn for himself if she couldn't fork over the funds.

Her shoulders slumped, and she lifted Baby into her arms, accepting her comforting doggy licks. Autumn's vision to match trained service dogs with people in need was vanishing.

"Hey there," Wyatt said as he stepped into the booth. "Where's Harper?" His gaze roamed the area.

She blinked and searched behind her. "She was just here." Autumn's chest tightened. Why hadn't she been paying closer attention to Harper's whereabouts?

"You've lost her?" He flashed Autumn a look, and all she could see was disappointment, as though appalled at her lack of responsibility. "I never should have trusted you with my daughter." His voice rose with each word, but she didn't care if everyone overheard. She deserved his anger.

"I'm so sorry," she whispered. But he didn't seem to hear her as he turned and rushed off to find Harper.

A lump the size of Texas formed in Autumn's throat at losing track of Harper. Where could she have run off to?

Autumn pressed Baby close, breathing in her canine companion's familiar smell.

Why had she thought she could ever be a positive role model for anyone? Her stomach twisted at the turn of events. Harper was missing right now because of Autumn's carelessness.

Wyatt's last words resounded in her ears. *I never should have trusted you.* Her gut clenched tighter as guilt tangled around the knot already formed there. He was right. If Harper hadn't been left in her care, the sweet girl wouldn't be missing.

Wyatt rushed through the town square and kept his eyes peeled for Harper. Where was she? How could Autumn have lost her?

An invisible fist squeezed the breath out of his lungs. Why had he relied on Autumn to care for his child? Trusting his mother was one thing, but Autumn? What had he been thinking by letting down his guard?

He shook off his annoyance with Autumn, because right now, the only thing that mattered was finding his daughter. It wasn't like Harper to go off on her own.

His feet pounded across the pavement as he scanned the children in the crowds. He was desperate to catch sight of his daughter and her oversized navy T-shirt advertising Autumn's business. He was trying to cover ground swiftly, yet be careful not to overlook her. Could someone have kidnapped her? His eyes rounded in surprise. No. This was Serenity. She was safe, right?

Then he gazed at the sea of people, many strangers and nonresidents here for the day. An overwhelming sense of dread came over him, then fear sprouted and wound around his chest.

He shouldn't have left Autumn in charge of his daughter, never should have trusted her. He stopped at the end of the square and roughed a hand over his face. Right then he spotted a little girl about Harper's height sporting a long blue T-shirt.

Hope surged, and he sprinted over, but at the last moment she turned and it wasn't Harper after all. The shirt didn't even have any lettering on it. He held back a frustrated scream of helplessness. The adrenaline that had been shooting through his system dropped off and his body began to shake. He gasped, but pushed on. Where was Harper?

Maybe he should call the police. He pulled out his phone but then shuddered at the time it would take away from his search. Surely she was in the crowds nearby. He kept searching.

Harper just had to be okay. A clot of emotion tried to take over, but he pushed it away. She had to be around here somewhere.

Lord, please. Keep my baby safe until she's back in my arms.

His gaze caught on the colorful festival games and he darted that way, hoping Harper had gotten distracted by the festive games.

He spied a girl with long brown hair, her small hand gripped by a beefy man. *Abducted. No!* Wyatt's heart crushed in panic as he raced to them and jerked the man away from the girl. When he saw the surprised faces of unfamiliar people, Wyatt backed away, hands up as he apologized for his rash behavior.

He stepped away from the two, his clammy hands trembling. His breath burst in and out as though he'd just run a marathon. Full-fledged terror replaced his panic, and he realized he had no choice but to call the police. He pulled his phone out and with shaking fingers began to make the call.

"Wyatt," someone called his name. He turned and saw Harper holding hands with Cora. Sweet relief seized him as he pocketed his phone and rushed to his daughter, picked her up and squeezed tight. *Thank you, Lord.*

"She was wandering around without you or Autumn or your mother, so I thought it'd be best to find one of you," the older woman said.

"Thank you, Cora." He choked down the grateful lump in his throat.

Autumn's mother gave a little wave and walked away.

"Daddy, you're squeezing too hard," Harper said. He almost whimpered at her adorable voice.

He placed his daughter on the ground and knelt in front of her. "Sweetheart, you can't roam around without an adult. At least, not in crowds this size. I was worried about you." His chin trembled at the thought of losing her. When he'd been on the hunt, he'd been able to keep his emotions in check. But now that she was standing right here, his mind was spinning with all the horrible possibilities that thankfully hadn't happened.

"But Miss Autumn wouldn't play ring toss with me like she promised." She pouted. "I asked and asked and asked, but she was too busy talking about dogs to everyone. Then I asked her and she finally nodded, so I took off, thinking she was behind me. I'm sorry, Daddy."

So Autumn had given Harper the impression they were leaving, when in fact she was preoccupied with potential clients. She'd made the choice to put growing her business over the safety of his daughter.

Wyatt pressed his eyes closed as anger over the incident surged. He hadn't been there and had left Autumn in charge of his child.

He had relied on her. Believed leaning on her was a good thing. Clearly, he had been wrong.

He gave Harper a quick hug, then popped her on his hip. "I was looking for you because we need to leave."

"Aw, Daddy, I want to stay." She placed her head on his shoulder as though she sensed he wasn't in the mood for a debate.

He wove around the crowds toward his truck. He had trusted his gut when he'd met and married Chloe and look how horribly that had turned out. Was trusting Autumn wrong too?

His instincts for reading and assessing people might be off because his ex-wife had made selfish decisions, similar to what Autumn did today. Did Autumn have a bit of his ex-wife in her? He shivered at the notion.

Seemed she thought parenting was all fun and games until it messed with her cherished business life.

His heart squeezed in anguish.

He recalled Autumn's face when he'd told her he shouldn't have trusted her with Harper. He lifted his chin. Since his daughter had been found safe and sound, he might have over-reacted. No, today was a reminder that he didn't have the right to open up his life to someone else, not when Harper's safety was involved.

How had he gotten swept up in a romance with Autumn so quickly? He shook his head. He had no idea, but this was the very reason he had never wanted to be in another relationship again.

The past had taught him that others would always abuse his trust, so it was better to keep his distance. Why had he believed in love again and let down his guard?

He had no choice but to protect his heart, and more importantly, Harper's.

He unlocked the truck and situated a sleepy Harper in her car seat, placing a kiss on her soft cheek.

As long as he didn't trust anyone other than his mother with his precious daughter, nothing like this could happen again.

He needed to put distance between himself and Autumn. Which meant he'd have to come up with a good reason to move away from the Triple C.

Autumn had been alone with Harper for half an hour, and she hadn't been able to keep tabs on her. Regret knifed her, but she had to hold her emotions in, at least until she returned to the privacy of the Triple C.

Since the festival was almost over and Wyatt was no longer around, there was no need to stay. She began to assemble her belongings to leave. She didn't think she could handle one more person stopping to ask if they'd found Harper. Her mother had come by to tell her what had happened and that the sweet girl was in Wyatt's very capable arms.

Ever since the celebratory dinner at the diner, Autumn had been contemplating if she was good enough to be a bonus mom to Harper. Today proved she wasn't.

How hard was it to keep an eye on a cute little four-year-old? Not hard at all. But Autumn had failed. Thank God, Harper was safe.

She called Wyatt one more time, hoping he'd pick up so she could apologize, but the call went directly to voice mail.

She knew when she was being dismissed. And he had every right because she had no excuse. She recalled Harper tugging on her shorts and begging her to play ring toss like they'd planned. Why hadn't she paid closer attention to the tot?

Things had been going so well with Wyatt and Harper. Autumn should have realized they wouldn't last. Nothing did. Nothing of importance, anyway.

The past had taught her that she wasn't important enough for others to stick around.

She knew from the way he was handling her phone calls that he was done with her. Her chin trembled at no longer having them in her life. She should have known better than to lose her heart to Wyatt. And Harper.

"You aren't leaving, are you?" Trisha entered the tiny booth as Autumn threw the last of the flyers in her bag and gathered Baby into her arms.

"Yes. I think I've done enough for one day."

Trisha's face dropped. "Stuff like this happens with kids. It'll blow over, you'll see."

"No it won't," she said as she buried her nose in Baby's

fur. She'd have to be content with fur babies, because she'd never be a mother to a human child. Her heart sank in her chest as the fact crystallized. Then she recalled nodding to Harper amid the tense conversation with Tyler and contemplated how the little girl may have misinterpreted the gesture. She pressed her lips into a thin line at her colossal mistake.

"I remember Harper pleading with me," Autumn said, her voice shaky at the memory. "She was standing on that chair right there. When she asked if we could go to the ring toss, I nodded, but I didn't mean anything by it. Tyler was here and I was trying to get him to understand how important the dog barn was to my business. I think Harper misunderstood and thought I was ready to leave."

Tears swam in her eyes as she swung her bag over her shoulder and stepped around her sister-in-law.

"Sweetie," Trisha said as she touched Autumn's arm and made her stop.

If only Autumn could have a redo for today. She would have made her intentions clear by telling Harper that they would leave as soon as her father returned.

She sighed and waited for whatever nugget Trisha had for her. The woman was meant to be a mother. It came as naturally as walking to her. Last year, she had taken three orphans under her wing as though it wasn't a massive life change for all of them.

"It'll work out. Harper is just fine, and Wyatt will realize he never should have said those things to you."

Autumn turned to face her sister-in-law, who'd become a good friend over the past year, and pressed Baby a little closer to her chest. "Wyatt was right. I truly don't know what we were thinking pursuing each other. I'm not cut out to be a mother figure. It doesn't come natural to me like it does you."

Before Trisha could respond, Autumn turned and fled to the sanctuary of her old SUV. Wyatt's words, *I never should have trusted you with my daughter*, resounding in her head on repeat. His truthful words reverberated in the small space.

A hollow ache settled in her core. He was so right. Seven years ago, she'd decided she'd make a terrible mother. Today reminded her that she was the same person. Nothing had miraculously changed through the years.

Chapter Fifteen

A week later, Wyatt slipped out of his bed in the early morning and headed to Nana's kitchen and the enticing smell of brewing coffee. His mother sat at the bistro table, nursing a cup of steaming java.

"Good morning, sweetheart," she said, a bright smile on her tired face. "Did you sleep well?"

"Yes," he said, even though all he'd done was toss and turn, like every night since they'd moved back into Nana's cramped two bedroom apartment.

Even though he knew it was the right and only thing to do, his decision to keep Harper away from Autumn was weighing on his mind. They hadn't spoken since the day of the festival. He'd replied to Autumn's frantic text messages to let her know he'd found his daughter, and she was safe. He longed for things to return to the way they were, a simple and carefree budding relationship with Autumn, but he wasn't sure that would be the best for himself or Harper.

Keeping their distance from Autumn would protect from future disappointments. He wasn't sure either of them had it in them to weather another storm like they had with Chloe. Even though his heart wrenched with his fearfulness, he didn't feel as though he had a choice.

He settled at the chair across from his mother, a hot cup

of caffeinated bliss in his hands. The cloudy day matched his miserable mood. "Thanks for putting up with us, Mom. I know Nana would probably sleep and rest better if we weren't here, but I just can't find anywhere else in Serenity that we can afford. I mean, I have that debt from Chloe that isn't going anywhere, so my budget is pretty restricted."

She covered his hand with hers. "You are welcome here for as long as you like, but sweetheart, Harper was upset again last night that she couldn't be at the Triple C while you were training the dogs. She cried herself to sleep." His mother's hand retreated as she took a sip of her coffee.

And his daughter had woken twice with nightmares. Just when things had been going well, now everything was out of whack again.

He sat back in his chair, the hard metal pressing into his back muscles. "Mom, you know my stance. I never should have trusted Autumn with Harper. It was a mistake. Now, I'm doing the best I can, backpedaling with Harper. She's better off without Autumn in her life." But a niggle of doubt crept into his mind. Instead of pushing it away, he let it linger and allowed himself to consider all his options.

"Is she? Because day care started calling you again to pick Harper up early."

"She's just going through an adjustment," he snapped. Regret over his sharp words pinched his chest. "I'm sorry about that, Mom, but you know I'm a born fixer."

"Honey, you can't fix everything. But you can hand it over to God and rest in Him."

He believed in God, but struggled with giving it all to Him and not stepping in to help. Maybe now was time to start. He shrugged off the notion, because he needed to focus on getting through his day, not second-guessing a necessary decision he'd made.

"I know I can rest in God, but you don't seem to understand that Autumn put her own needs over Harper's well-being. I've been with someone like that before and look how it turned out."

"But, sweetheart, Harper could have snuck away had she been with anyone. Even you or me. It wasn't Autumn's fault."

He glared at his mother. "Listen, Autumn put making money and advancing her business over the safety of my child. Your granddaughter. How can you be on her side?"

"Wyatt, there are no sides." She wrapped her hands around her mug, which had to be lukewarm by now. "Accidents happen. That's the definition of the word *accident*."

He stilled, allowing his mother's wisdom to soak in. He'd been steeped in righteous anger ever since the festival and hadn't been able to think clearly. His initial panic and subsequent outrage at Autumn's actions had dissipated as the days had passed.

Was he making too much about Harper running off while under Autumn's care? He didn't want to agree with his mother, but part of him conceded that, given the right motivation, Harper might have snuck away no matter who was watching her. Even him.

Doubt coursed through him.

"Still, I never should have allowed Autumn to become such an integral part of our lives," he said. "After Chloe became addicted to drugs and was not dependable to provide a safe place for Harper, I learned that trusting a woman was wrong." He took a sip of his steaming coffee, but it didn't satisfy like it usually did. "With all that Dad put you through, you know exactly how I feel. I'm sure if you could do it over again, you wouldn't have let him into your life."

"Oh no, I disagree. If it weren't for your father, I wouldn't have you. I wouldn't have Harper. I wouldn't know and rely on my Lord as heavily as I do." Her gaze pierced him. "Hard things happen in life, but He got me through that time, and I walked out with you and a strong relationship with God.

"One bad relationship," she continued, "doesn't mean you give up on women forever. It means you learn and grow and make sure future relationships are healthy. From what I can tell, Autumn is a woman after God. She loves you and Harper deeply, and she is an upstanding woman who'd do anything to keep you and Harper loved and safe."

His mother's words wound around his core and found truth and somehow a bit of healing from his experiences with his ex-wife. Yes, he needed to move on in his life and move forward. He didn't want Harper to focus on the negativity of her mother for the rest of her life, just like he shouldn't dwell on the disaster of a marriage he and Chloe had shared.

"I'm going to wake up Nana. We need to leave the house in an hour for an appointment, and it takes a while to get her moving." His mother left the room. Her wisdom clinging to the air molecules whizzing around him.

Was he right to push Autumn away from Harper? And himself?

He wasn't sure.

The answers hinged on whether he could he trust a woman again.

And he wasn't sure he could.

The overcast day matched Autumn's discouraged attitude of late. Thankfully, her sister-in-law had invited her on a trail ride at Serenity Stables to take her mind off her woes. Autumn had been so busy these past few months she hadn't found the occasion to ride or spend much time with Trisha, who'd been slowly becoming her best friend.

"How many times do I have to tell you, Autumn? It wasn't your fault," Trisha responded as she twisted in her saddle to make eye contact. But the words didn't make Autumn feel better at all.

"Wyatt trusted me to watch his child, and I lost her. That's nothing to sneeze at."

Trisha huffed. "It could have happened with anyone."

"But it was with *me*," Autumn stated, her throat tight with emotion. "You know about Wyatt's past and how he struggles with trust. I don't think he'll ever be able to forgive me."

"Just give him time," Trisha said. "I've seen the three of you together and you've seamlessly stepped into the bonus mom role. You're a natural."

Autumn was thankful Wyatt had come back into her life and forced her to deal with the emotions she tried for years to sweep under the rug. Because now, being a mom was something she wanted. "You think so?"

"Yes. You have a strong maternal instinct."

Autumn allowed her friend's words to soak in. Was Trisha right?

"Stop beating yourself up over what happened," Trisha said. Autumn's horse lifted his head and shook as though agreeing.

As they approached the pond, Autumn sat straighter in the saddle. Her friend was right. She needed to put this behind her, and so did Wyatt.

If only he could get past his trust issues.

They stopped at the pond. Autumn swung her leg over the saddle and dropped to the ground, feeling freer now than she had in a very long time. Since Wyatt had come to town, the burden of holding her pregnancy and miscarriage secret had ended. And the wall she'd erected between her and her family because of that secret had crumbled.

They loosely tied the horse's reins to the hitching post, then Autumn picked up a few flat stones. She took a seat on the edge of the water. Trisha settled beside her.

All along, Autumn had believed she'd never make a good mother, but that was a lie she had told herself when she was twenty-one because she was so fearful of another miscarriage.

She tossed a stone; it bounced off the surface of the pond three times before sinking.

"I could never skip rocks."

"Helps to grow up with four brothers."

Autumn leaned back on her elbows.

Maybe, just maybe, given the chance, she could be a solid bonus-mom for Harper. Hope rose in her chest.

"Do you have any leads for another place to rent?"

Autumn sighed at the troublesome topic. "No. I've reached out to everyone I know. Just like a year ago, Henry's is the only option."

"We've been praying. I'm confident God will provide."

Maybe, but Autumn was superfrustrated. She'd worked so hard to get Henry to agree to her using that empty barn only to have the rules change partway through playing the game.

Her phone buzzed. She looked at the display and sucked in a breath. "It's Morgan," she said, grateful they'd exchanged numbers at the festival. She answered.

"Listen Autumn, I am so sorry about the fuss during the festival and how my brother made a snap decision about renting you the dog barn."

Adrenaline rushed through her body at the implication. Was Tyler going to allow her to use the dog barn?

"I've talked with him and he's calmed down. In fact, if you and Wyatt can supply our nephew with a trained support dog by Christmas, Tyler will allow you to continue renting his space and waive the rent for a year. Can you train a dog that quickly?"

"Yes, we can!" Autumn said, even though she wasn't sure if Wyatt was still working for her or if he'd even be able to train new dogs.

"I'm so relieved. My nephew just had an episode yesterday and even though he's fine, he really needs some support going forward."

"Thanks, Morgan. I really appreciate this opportunity."

"No, thank you. Our nephew needs help and to be honest, we don't have plans to use the dog barn anyway. I simply love your vision of matching trained dogs with people in need."

After profusely thanking her again. Autumn disconnected the call.

"Congratulations," Trisha said as she leaned in for a tight hug. She must have heard the whole conversation.

Autumn's eyes teared up, thrilled she could keep using the dog barn. She was optimistic her business would succeed. Whether she'd have Wyatt as her trainer, she had no idea.

"I need to get back, sorry." Trisha rose and brushed off her jeans.

They both mounted their horses, and Autumn's mind turned back to Wyatt and how upset he was with her. She and Trisha rode side by side in the open field. "I broke Wyatt's trust."

"So take matters into your hands," she stated, almost like a stern warning. "Make him see he's wrong and that it could have happened to anyone."

Right then, Autumn noticed that she and her horse had made a shadow on the field of Texas bluebonnets. She looked into the sky and saw that the heavy clouds had moved away and the sun shone brighter than she'd ever seen. The sudden change of weather gave her hope.

Her pulse quickened at the thought of apologizing. Of making up. Of having them back in her life.

She glanced at Trisha, who'd gone through a lot to move from a secure academic life in Iowa to running a horse stable and married to a sudden-dad with three young children. But she had taken the leap and look at how fulfilled she was.

Autumn's heart yearned to have Wyatt back in her life. Could Autumn ever have what she wanted—a happily ever after with Wyatt and Harper?

She nodded as she decided if she ever got a second chance with him, she'd take it and never look back. She'd had it with second-guessing her life. It was time to live.

"So, are you going to do it? Take the bull by the horns and let Wyatt know how you feel?" Trisha asked.

Autumn set her jaw. Yes, tonight when he arrived to train the dogs, she wouldn't give him the space he'd asked for. Instead, she'd approach him and give him one last apology. Hopefully, he'd accept it and at least let her back into his and Harper's life—even if they couldn't have a romantic relationship. She wanted to be a part of his life again and for things to get back to some kind of normal she could live with.

But she hoped they could have more.

At lunch time, Doc Earl had a special event with his wife, so he had given Wyatt an extra long mid-day break. They were so close with Tallulah that Wyatt wanted to devote a little more time with her, so he drove over to the Triple C Ranch.

When he pulled into the parking area, there were no

parking spots available. Cora and Wade must have been having a get together. He settled his truck in the overflow lot where employees parked and deliveries were made and trudged over to the dog barn.

He had a successful session with Tallulah. After he returned the dog to her crate, he noticed all the cars were gone and Autumn's older SUV was there.

Would she come over? His heart stuttered at the chance to see her. She'd been keeping a respectful distance ever since the festival, but was that what he wanted?

Talking with his mother this morning clarified things about his father. Wyatt recalled when his father had dragged him into his cheating scheme, never allowing Wyatt to say a word. But Wyatt wasn't a kid anymore. His father no longer controlled him. His mother was out from under his father's thumb and happily tending to Nana's needs. Even though it had been painful in the moment, all that had worked out. He and his mother had walked away unscathed.

His mother had put her husband's cheating behind her and moved forward to thrive. Wyatt needed to follow her example and stop allowing his childhood wounds to define him.

He lifted the lid of the small metal garbage container on the wall and disposed of the scented cotton balls he'd used for Tallulah's training. He dropped the lid and it clanged shut.

His father and Chloe had burned bridges with the way they'd treated him, but Autumn hadn't done anything of the sort. His mother was right. She'd made a mistake that frankly he could have made.

Maybe Harper running off like that hadn't been Autumn's fault. Maybe, like his mother said, no one was to blame.

But could he risk his and Harper's hearts again? He wasn't

sure. It'd be safer to clear the air with Autumn and go back to just friend status. He nodded. He liked safe.

His phone rang. When he saw the display, his heart sank. Day care. He answered.

Harper was inconsolable. Again. The director asked if he could pick her up. He turned and hurried to his truck.

As he rushed through the trodden grass, his well-worn boots clomped with each urgent step. His mind catalogued the past week, and he realized that after a month of sleep filled nights, Harper was having night terrors again. After a month of successful stints at day care, she was back to having difficulty again.

The only difference was Autumn's absence. He'd ripped Autumn from her the day of the festival with no explanation.

Here he was, attempting to shield Harper from getting hurt when, in fact, she was already shredded.

He was trying to protect Harper by removing a wonderful woman from her life. Someone who could make a fabulous mother for his daughter.

Like his mother had said earlier, Autumn loved him and Harper deeply. Even though it was scary, he loved her right back. Truth be told, he didn't want their breakup to be final.

His mother was so wise. Harper could have taken off on anyone's watch. Autumn had done nothing malicious.

He had to apologize and right this wrong.

But this time he needed to leave doubt in the rearview mirror because he and Harper adored Autumn.

He grinned as the heaviness in his chest he'd felt since Harper went missing vanished. As soon as dinner ended, he'd return to the Triple C, find Autumn and ask if she could ever forgive him for his foolish behavior.

He had been shortsighted to compare Autumn to his ex-wife. They were nothing alike. If Autumn gave him another shot, they'd start fresh, just like Autumn deserved.

That evening, right after a quick dinner at Nana's with his little family, Wyatt pulled in front of the McCaws' home. He looked up at his adorable garage apartment that had been vacant since the festival. In the dwindling daylight hours, motion on the McCaw wide front porch caught his attention. Autumn was perched on the edge of a rocking chair.

When their gazes collided, her face lit up and his pulse raced at her positive acknowledgment of him. He smiled, but his gripped hands never left the safety of the steering wheel.

He'd picked up Harper early and taken the afternoon off from the vet clinic. Once she was back at Nana's, his daughter had slept most of the afternoon. The extra time had allowed Wyatt to pray over his relationship with Autumn and read his Bible. His time with God had given him a peace that surpassed all understanding.

He dropped his hands and head.

Lord, thank you for showing me the error in my ways and giving me such peace today. Thank you for walking through this with me. Thank you for showing me that Autumn is not Chloe and that Autumn is worthy of my trust.

Confident in all the Lord had taught him, yet apprehensive about whether Autumn would accept his apology, he strode to the porch and pocketed his keys. He'd made the right decision to talk with her, but he was unsure what her response would be.

If she'd have him, he could see forever with her.

He stopped on the bottom step. "Can we talk?"

She nibbled her bottom lip as she nodded, eagerness covering her face. Her enthusiastic reaction made him believe this day might very well end with Autumn in his arms and a happily ever after.

He climbed the steps and then leaned against the post, not wanting to invade her personal space if she was still mad at him, which she had every right to be.

These next few minutes might define the rest of his life, so he had to be careful with what words he chose. He prayed for God to soften her heart to him, to hear him and to forgive him for being such a fool by allowing his trust issues to lead his life.

"Hi," she said, worry dancing in her eyes. He yearned to run a finger down her cheekbone to wipe the anxiety off her face. But for now, he kept his hands pocketed.

"I need to—" she said.

"I wanted—" he said at the same moment.

He smiled. At least she was talking to him. That was a good sign.

"If you don't mind, I have something I need to say," he said. She gave him a friendly nod that encouraged him to take a step closer. He had to lay it all out on the line and pray she'd accept his desperate plea. "I'm so sorry for saying what I did to you at the festival."

"I'm sorry about Harp—" She stopped when he raised his hand and then nodded for him to continue.

His heart thumped harder as she stood and took a step closer to him.

"She could have slipped away under anyone's care, Autumn. It wasn't your fault." Her lips pressed together as if she were trying to hold her words in. He reached for her hand and his skin tingled at the touch. "My mother reminded me that part of being a parent is dealing with adversities, and I didn't handle this one well at all."

When she ran her thumb along the back of his, hope took flight in his belly. "Please forgive me for what I said and for how I've treated you since the festival."

"Oh, Wyatt." Tears shimmered in her gorgeous emerald green eyes. "I was never mad at you, actually just the opposite. I was upset with myself for losing track of Harper. I guess when I got pregnant at twenty-one, I convinced myself I couldn't be a good mother because I was so young and still had a lot of growing up to do." She licked her perfectly kissable lips. "But I guess that time just instilled a lie in me that I've believed ever since. So when Harper got lost on my watch, I was convinced you were right and I couldn't possibly be a proper maternal influence in her life."

His love for her grew at her noble concern for Harper. "You're so wrong, Autumn. You are a great influence on my daughter. She adores you, and I love that she is looking up to a woman who is driven and focused in life because those are qualities I want her to have when she's an adult."

From the dog barn, Baby barked and started racing toward them as though she had just noticed Wyatt's arrival. They both chuckled at her antics as she flew onto the porch and insisted on some loving from him. He leaned down and ruffed up the Jack Russell's fur and let the terrier lick his face a few times.

"She loves you."

"Well, I love her." He stood and placed his attention solely on Autumn. Every time he looked into her heart-shaped face, he loved her more. "And her momma."

Autumn sucked in a breath as he twined his fingers through hers and pulled her closer. "I love you," he said, "more than I've ever loved anyone. If you're still interested, I'd really like to keep spending time with you and see where this relationship might lead." He had a strong feeling she was the one God had set aside for him.

"Oh, Wyatt, I'd like nothing more."

She threw her arms around him, and he kissed her.

This was the life he'd always wanted. A solid job, enjoyable hobbies, a happy daughter and a woman by his side that he loved spending time with. Autumn had made him the happiest man on earth.

She leaned back, their hands intertwined. "I never thought this would happen." Their gazes locked, and he tumbled into the passion and certainty he spied on her face.

"Autumn, you mean the world to me." Her grin in response told him everything he needed to know.

"Who would have thought that when we reconnected six weeks ago that you'd steal my heart and be the forever someone I didn't know I was looking for?"

He couldn't stop beaming. "I never thought I'd fall in love again. Never thought I'd be able to trust again. But God knew different. He helped me open my heart to another romance. I'm so glad He did, because I couldn't imagine the rest of my life, the rest of Harper's life, without you in it."

She made a happy noise and then melted against his chest.

He wrapped his arms around the love of his life and tucked her head under his chin, unable to wipe the sappy grin off his face. "Autumn, this is our second chance at love and I want to spend the rest of my life loving you."

Epilogue

Six months later, on their wedding day, Wyatt led Autumn down the flagstone trail toward Laney's rustic barn, where their reception would be. Her heart was full, fuller than she'd ever imagined it would be. The ceremony had been held on the bluff overlooking the rippling creek. The late afternoon sun had peeked through the mature oak trees, lending a romantic feel to the day as she took in her gorgeous husband's face and recited her wedding vows.

He squeezed her hand, and she gazed up into his chocolate eyes that sparkled with affection. She grinned at him and mouthed *elephant shoes*. He chuckled at the phrase Harper had learned in day care. If you mouth the phrase, it appears you are saying *I love you*. She adored she was part of this little family and their inside jokes.

"See Baby? She got her vest dirty," Harper said as she rolled her eyes. Baby, her pink ring bearer vest filthy, stood next to Harper and cocked her head. At least she had waited until after the ceremony to roll in dirt.

Autumn pushed an errant lock of hair behind Harper's ear. Her hairstyle was perfect for her age, the curls and crown of baby's breath suited her to a tee. As soon as Harper saw her cousins, Zoe and Tori, she took off to play tag with them.

"After Chloe left, I thought it'd be just the two of us. Now she has a mother and all the McCaws to call family." As he stared after his daughter, he rubbed Autumn's thumb.

She thanked God for opening up their hearts to a relationship and allowing them to trust each other. And for healing the wounds Harper carried from her mother. Autumn's chest gave a tight squeeze at the amazing changes all three of them had gone through these past few months.

After the informal dinner came the first dance. A nervous yet excited feeling shimmered in Autumn's core. The celebration had flown by and she wanted to cherish every moment of their special day.

"Mr. and Mrs. Wyatt Nelson," the DJ introduced them.

Butterflies took flight in her belly as Wyatt lifted her hand and led her under the large white tent to the makeshift dance floor. The crowd roared at the introduction and their appearance. She beamed. Her cheeks hurt from the excessive smiling, but she couldn't help it. He placed his hands on her waist and she wrapped her arms around his strong neck and they swayed to the music.

"I love you," she whispered.

"Love you more," he responded with a satisfied sigh.

She pressed her cheek against her husband's capable chest, so grateful for him and the love they now shared. The first time he'd walked up the little dog barn hill, she had believed her life was about to come crashing down on her. Instead, his presence had healed her broken past. In fact, she hadn't known what she had been missing until handsome Wyatt and sweet Harper had entered her world. Now she couldn't imagine her life without them.

"In half a year, I've gone from a single woman afraid to trust and love to a married mother," she said, attempting to keep the happy tears at bay. "I've never felt so blessed."

He pressed a kiss on her forehead as the DJ announced everyone could join the happy couple.

Harper rushed at them, Baby and Buster not far behind. Wyatt had adopted the border collie for his daughter shortly after he and Autumn had kissed and made up after the festival incident. Harper had thrived having a dog all her own. Wyatt lifted their daughter and popped her on his hip so they could have a family dance. Harper wrapped her arms around both their necks with a squeal.

"This is so much fun," she declared, then pushed her head forward so their three foreheads touched. "I'm so glad you're my mommy."

Autumn swallowed against the sudden, happy lump in her throat at the little girl's words. She was a mommy now! *Thank you, Lord.* She never thought this would happen and here she was, a mommy to the best little girl in the world. It didn't matter how old Autumn got, she'd never tire of hearing Harper calling her *Mommy* and being Harper's mom.

"Look, my cousins," Harper said with pride as she spotted Tori and Zoe. She wriggled out of Wyatt's grasp to join her new family members.

Wyatt closed the gap between them as Autumn took in his features. His now grown-out hair had a cute wave to it when it got too long and his sun-darkened skin and lean, muscled arms spoke to his hardworking lifestyle. She leaned her head against her dreamy husband's able shoulder.

This man, who she'd been angry at, had turned into her hero and the man of her dreams. They'd healed together, both learned to trust again, and their relationships with the Lord had grown so much since their romance began.

"I've been thinking," Wyatt said. "How about we build a house on the plot of land your parents have set aside for you?"

Excitement bubbled up at the forever life they were stepping into. The countless decisions they'd make as a team. "Yes, I'd love that, Wyatt." He grinned at her and her heart thundered in her chest.

For years she'd lived in a holding pattern, unable to forget the past and step into the present. But now the past was where it belonged and their future was so bright it blinded her.

"I was thinking," he whispered in her ear, tickling the sensitive spot on her neck. "Maybe we could fill our new house up with a passel of kids."

"Oh, Wyatt, nothing would make me happier."

* * * * *

Dear Reader,

Thank you for joining me on Autumn and Wyatt's journey in Serenity, Texas, my third installment of the Triple C Ranch Series.

The inspiration for this story comes from my love of Jack Russell Terrier dogs, specifically rescues. I admire the communities that rally around breeds and rescue them from many places, including shelters, so that people can adopt these sweet dogs and give them a second chance at a forever home.

I hope you enjoyed this story as much as I did. Watching these two characters reconnect now that they are more mature and new creations in Christ was neat to watch unfold. I especially like how Wyatt, a born fixer, learns he can't fix everything and that he must surrender and rest in God.

It would be fantastic to connect with you. Drop me a note at http://heidimain.com. While there, you can sign up for my newsletter for book news, giveaways and life reports.

Hugs,
Heidi